THE
NIHILESTHETE

by

Richard Kalich

The Permanent Press, Sag Harbor, New York 11963

For my brother, Robert Kalich

Library of Congress Number: 86-062449
International Standard Book Number: 1-57962079-5

Manufactured in the United States of America

THE PERMANENT PRESS
RD2 Noyac Road
Sag Harbor, NY 11963

Case Record
of
Robert Haberman, Caseworker

Apologia

I write these notes for what they are worth . . . for me.
Under no circumstances, in any shape, manner or form,
were they intended . . . for you. They were written and
kept solely for the singular joy I received from them;
and—the most important reason—for what they added to
my original experience and thought.

In no way should they be considered true indicia of what
they depict. For what they depict is me. My life's blood is
the ink . . . these pages merely frame, place and perhaps
help circulate the words. If, perchance, these pages do fall
into your hands, please do not be so quick to judge. Not
my words, MY LIFE! That is the important thing. The
rest, these futile scribblings, they are mere artifice. Despite
all my efforts, it would be folly to think I could ever
capture the fecundity of my moods with words.

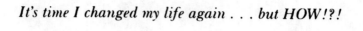

It's time I changed my life again . . . but HOW!?!

Something interesting happened to me today. As I was walking home from the subway after work, I stopped to watch an artist draw a picture of Christ on the sidewalk in front of the Maine Monument. There was a crowd surrounding the artist, but one area was left open purposefully. This visual corridor was to accommodate a limbless figure in a wheelchair who was also watching the event. It wasn't long before the wheelchair-bound figure came to dominate my attention.

It was immediately evident that he was some sort of retard, a freak of the kind I had seen just a few nights earlier on a TV expose program. He certainly didn't have the slightest idea what was going on around him. I could tell this by the fact that he didn't adjust himself in any way to the dogs, pigeons, squirrels, even the kids romping about. One child nearly landed in his lap (if he had a lap) when his Frisbee knocked into the retard's chest. Nothing seemed to disturb him or penetrate his consciousness. Except The Artist and her Drawing!

When I accidentally moved into his path just before leaving, I could swear I noticed a pained expression come over his face, or a grimace of defiance. And also, I think—I couldn't be sure at the time—I heard him make a mewing sound like a cat's cry.

As I continued on home I persuaded myself it was just an idiot's reaction and was prepared to forget it. I had even begun to warm my supper up and was, as usual, watching the 6 o'clock news, when I realized I couldn't. The image of the retard's face kept flickering before my eyes, intruding itself on the TV screen. And so despite my weariness, and customary unbending attitude to changing my regimen, I decided to return to the Maine Monument. While getting dressed and walking there, I remember being unable to shake the feeling of being a criminal returning to the scene of the crime.

As fate would have it, the retard was still there when I arrived. The crowd had dispersed, and the artist had just finished collecting the last of her art supplies and was now busily engaged in tallying up her earnings for the day. I waited patiently for her to finish and strode briskly up to her sketch at the precise moment she was taking her leave. Strangely, or maybe not so strangely, the retard lapsed into silence the second he saw me. No more mewing sounds came from his direction. And though I gave every appearance of doing no more than admiring the artist's drawing, even positioning myself in such a way so as not to interfere with his line of vision, in reality I never took my eyes off the freak.

Likewise, I could feel his boring into me.

Almost immediately I came upon a plan of action. Why or what motivated me I can't really say. Call it premonition . . . some blind instinct . . . but in my own way I knew what I was doing. I stepped on the drawing. As it was done in chalk, I was fully cognizant of the effect my shoe would have on the creation. AND SO WAS HE!!! It was just as I expected—the moment the sole of my shoe touched the sketch, the same pained expression appeared on the retard's face. And he made the same mewing sound. It was evident he was RESPONDING! We were like two implacable enemies on opposite sides of the arena, each making ready to do battle over his most prized and precious turf. Each recognizing the other for what he was. I was about to go over to the man and take a closer look when a woman emerged as if from nowhere and whisked him away. By the time I regrouped from my moment's hesitation, they were gone.

That evening I tossed and turned in my sleep.
Needless to say something was brewing inside me.
I promised myself I would try again the next day.

He was not there the next day nor the next day nor the next. I am in the doldrums. I have nothing but my job and my apartment. They are not enough. I go on looking.

4

NEW YORK MEDICAL CENTER
Institute of Rehabilitation Medicine
800 East 34th Street, New York, N.Y.
Area (212) 679-0000
Cable Address: NYU MEDIC

Nov. 28, 1985

Director, Dept. of Social Services
Dept. 29
765 East 126th St.
New York, New York

RE: BRODSKI
d.o.b.
3/18/61
IPM Chart
#29205

Dear Sir:

We are referring the case of BRODSKI, (no known first name), a 24 year-old single unattached male, to your agency for possible service. Brodski has been cared for all his life by Mrs. Maria Rivera, a woman who refers to herself as his mother. Actually she is not blood related but only assumed responsibility when his actual mother (unknown) abandoned him at birth. Mrs. Rivera is 68 years of age and her health is deteriorating rapidly. She suffers from bursitis, arthritis, and C.V.A. Still, she is reluctant to have anyone but herself care for him and only because of his recent hospitalization has this case been brought to our attenion. If it were up to Mrs. Rivera, Brodski would remain in her care and no outside help would be requested from any agencies. It must be admitted that she has done an excellent job. When born, Brodski's life span was short and only through extraordinary mothering care has he been able to reach his present age. That is our medical staff's opinion.

5

The family resides in a two-room apartment with self-service elevator which gives easy access for his wheelchair.

Mrs. Rivera has been in receipt of social security since Brodski's birth and he receives SSI.

Brodski is a low grade idiot; additionally born with a rare condition: Cri du Chat syndrome. (This diagnosis is inexact or partial; our medical staff is still unclear about some aspects of his disease.) He has vestigial arms and legs. At birth he had a high-pitched, unnerving cry, closely resembling the cry of a cat, therefore the diagnosis. He is totally dependent in self-care activities. He should be turned at least twice during the night to prevent skin breakdown. He is in adult diapers and is transported by wheel chair.

We feel placement in a facility would bring about a rapid death. He now only responds to one person, Maria Rivera, but for his own good must be made receptive to others. We have explained this necessity to Mrs. Rivera. However, as suggested, she is a proud woman and fretful of having anyone come into her home and upset the relationship she has with her stepson. Understandably, she is overly protective. Whatever your agency decides, if possible, we would recommend that Mrs. Rivera remain with Brodski and continue to assume those responsibilities that her health permits.

It should be reiterated that it is just Mrs. Rivera's attitude regarding outside help that remains this case's greatest problem. Because of this, all outside agencies over the years have refused to get involved and the case has remained isolated. However, perhaps now, because of her own increasing years and the infirmities of age, as well as Brodksi's recent need for hospitalization, she might be more receptive to outside help. At least I hope so. In any case your agency should handle the matter most discreetly no matter what course of action you take.

There are no relatives, friends; no one to contact in case of emergency.

Our request is that you go in and do what you can, perhaps a part-time Home Attendant at first. In the meantime, Brodski will continue to receive Home Care visits from this hospital. Please let us know of your findings and assessment of the case as soon as possible.

We thank you kindly for your cooperation. If further information is needed, please do not hesitate to call me at 679-0000, extension 2372.

Sincerely Yours,

Thea Goldstein
Senior Social Worker

Gerald Umano, MD
Director, Out Patient Services

GU:ime

It's him! It's him! Who else can it be? "Lowgrade idiot, limbless . . . Cri du Chat." What luck. What coincidence. For two weeks now I've hunted all over for him in vain and now he shows up on my desk. What could be better? Though everything in me pines to rush out to him at once, I shall wait. The waiting will do me good. It will calm my anticipation and heighten it at the same time. Yes. Before visiting him I shall first have a good long lunch.

Meanwhile, I will perform my office duties as usual. Especially . . . as usual.

Ahhhh, for the first time in God knows how long, I feel good. Good! Lunch will be delectable. I shall savor every morsel.

I did not go into his room. I refused to see him. Though refused is too strong a word. Naturally I made proper apologies to "Mother." I explained that it was already late, that I was in a rush, having many more field visits scheduled for the afternoon. That tomorrow would be soon enough for meeting him. Today I merely wanted to meet her. To introduce myself. My agency's services.

What was that, Mother? You don't need services. Just more money. You can hardly pay the rent with the income you now have. Food prices are up and going even higher. No, no, it's not a joking matter. But why do you laugh so, then? A nervous giggle? And the way your ears perked when I mentioned that you could be getting paid for being his Home Attendant. I shall never forget that look. It's recorded indelibly, like everything else.

But enough. To be sure, I said I've intruded enough for one day. I must be off.

If only she knew how much I mean to intrude.

And, lo and behold, tomorrow is Saturday. It's not a working day. I have the entire weekend to plan my approach. Did the Almighty need more when He created the world?

For the first time in the longest, my weekend will be full.

Nothing is more difficult than the weekend. Television can take us so far, the telephone never rings, and one can manage just so many trips to the refrigerator. It is not being alone but being with ourselves that is the killer. An entire metaphysic of distraction has evolved to stave off this terminal disease. We jog, we eat, we watch television, we read the tabloids, we fornicate, we go to the movies, opera, bars, ballet, we rush to and fro, hither and yon, to the neighbors, the beaches, boutiques, discos, friends, brunch, bar b-que, the window, anything . . . just to get away from ourselves. By the time Monday morning comes

around, and the grunts and groans of pleasure have sub-
sided, though no one would ever admit it ("Yes, Harriet, I
had a wonderful weekend"), we are truly grateful to return
to our daily hells. Anything is better than being with ourselves.

But this weekend was different. I had Brodski. We were
as close as two lovers pawing each other through the night,
sweat pouring profusely from our maddening embrace.
For forty-eight hours I was with you, my sweet. I was as
content as a scientist peering through his microscope. Indeed I am developing my own special kind of myopia.
Brodski is on my slide. He is my cubic unit of measurement. Though I shall give him wings, he shall never fly.
Poor thing, he shall never fly.
What are his weaknesses? More importantly, what are his
strengths? His passions? Is he capable of perception? Rec-
ognition? Of forming a bond? Of extending trust? Of
having a r-e-l-a-t-i-o-n-s-h-i-p? If not, can he be made to do
so? Of course he can. And I will make him. This idiot who
responded to the artist's drawing and to nothing else . . .
but me. This idiot . . . that look . . . that gesture of defiance. Yes. There is life here. A glimmer. Something to
work with. To harvest and bear fruit.

Oh, my work is cut out for me. It won't be easy. It never
is. But it shall be done. There is none better at it than I.

I visited my pending case first thing Monday morning.
My stratgem was simple: to catch the old lady off guard.
Friday I left early, exhibiting, despite my apologies, just the
slightest hint of indifference. It wasn't. When I declined
my opportunity for seeing Brodski, I knew what I was
doing. I always know what I am doing. This morning I am
all eyes and ears. Everything about him is of interest to me.

9

I am deeply concerned. Nothing is irrelevant or takes too long to listen to. I want to see all, learn all, know all. The old lady doesn't know what to make of me. She is startled, baffled, confused. She is just where I want her. By being unsettled, she fixes her idea of me all the more firmly. In narrowing her perception of me, she opens me up. She believes anything is possible of me. What a strange man, she giggles to herself. Nothing could be better. Strange man, laughter. This is a good place to start . . . a relationship.

When I perused Mother's room Friday I was not impressed. All the usual welfare recipient's accoutrements were there—a hodgepodge of Woolworth's, Salvation Army junk stores, neighborhood furniture stores (selling everything on credit) and family memorabilia. Start with the prerequisite TV set (16 inches) and the mandatory photos of the Kennedy's and Martin Luther King atop the mantel. Then another photo in grainy brownwhite standing in arrears. Every item seen a thousand times in a thousand households on a thousand field visits by this caseworker. Plastic covers on the sofa and chair, smoked mirrors, furniture simulating some original design "downtown." And lest I forget: the obligatory crucifix and reassuring pious declarations ("In this house God dwells") and other hanging atrocities preaching the gospel of universal love. And a bureau with gilt-edged glass doors behind which huddled a bunched-up community of bric-a-brac, each relic perpetuating some ancient family tale. In sum, everything cheap, tasteless, functional, without style or elegance—unless, of course, you think the maxim "Cleanliness is next to godliness" still holds some semblance of value in today's world. Needless to say, I don't, but she does. Mother does. Good. Men like me thrive on simple souls like her. It makes our job easier.

When I arrived, Brodski was in the bath. Mother was giving her son his daily baptism. "Wonderful. Don't let me interrupt you," I said, making sure to avoid her dripping

10

hand. "Go right on with what you're doing, Mrs. Rivera. I'll only take a peek. No, not at Brodski. At his room. After all, he still has some rights, doesn't he? Modesty is fundamental to all human beings, is it not? And he is human, isn't he? Even if he is a . . . Yes, yes. I'll wait till you bring him out all fresh and clean. Puffed up and crinkly pink like freshly starched linen. No one wants to be seen in soiled clothes, you know. Least of all a man without arms and legs."

Mother smiles tenuously and continues about her business. Though seemingly happy and content, she doesn't know what to make of me. Or does she? When we are utterly confused, only the extreme reactions are possible. Either we set up massive security blocks or we give in altogether. The Jews in concentration camps proved that, among other things. Auschwitz was the breeding ground of mind-boggling feats of heroism and survival, and of succombing to fate without so much as a whimper. Personally I prefer a good battle. There's no real victory without it.

Brodski's room: It couldn't have been more interesting. I must admit I was caught completely unawares. In my wildest dreams I couldn't have imagined this paragon of style, proportion, form, taste, loveliness. Everything as it should be (or nearly). Brick walls, simulated antiques, fine reproductions of old paintings wonderfully selected, correctly placed, handsomely framed. Decorum, taste, subtlety, all are here. I don't know how to explain the contrast to Mother's room. After all, they live under the same roof, have the same decorator, have they not? But that's it. They don't! It's the only explanation possible. Brodski has decorated his own room. Somehow he has managed this. But how? I must find out. That among other things.

Before leaving his room I roll up his bamboo shade and take a quick look outside. Just as I suspected. The little devil saved the best view for himself. A marvelous vista. I'll wager that without having to be propped up one extra inch he can see across the river to Queens. Before returning to Mother's room to await Brodski, I snap the shade exactly back to place.

I seat myself on the old woman's sofa. At one time it might have served as a love seat, I think to myself. All in me is taut and tense. I am filled with the only excitement I know. I await Brodski.

How shall I appear? What should I say? All kinds of possibilities are open to me. Some have already been worked out, tested in earlier experiences. I am not unused to such things. Still, each time is different. Each time is new. The unknown is always there. The unpredictable. That is the challenge. The reason I am here.

Mother enters cradling her son in her arms. He is in some kind of homemade crib or casket, swathed in adult diapers. My first impression is of Pharoh's daughter carrying Moses from the river bed. Indeed, he is her Moses.

Brodski's head is small, maybe half that of a normal man, or a third, it's hard to say. Conical in shape. His features are either not there or swollen and distended from where they should be. Nothing is as it should be. At least not according to normal expectations. His ears are low set, not precisely even or paralleling each other. His mouth is that of a tiny bird. His nose is full, fleshy and much too large; it looks as if it was pressed on his face by a giant hand. His eyes are . . . his eyes are dead. They do not see. There is nothing behind them. Or at least so it seems to me . . . now. His hair line, as his chin, recedes. In fact, there is no chin. Just a little point protruding from his face. Certainly there is nothing you could describe as a jaw. His neck is also missing—rotund masses of skin webbing appear in its place. Altogether his face lacks harmony, the features are dissonant. Someone or something just threw them together for the fun of it. And he missed. But did he? Who's to say?

My first reaction is one of extreme joy and at the same time disappointment. Yes, disappointment. Because he does not recognize me. But then, he does not perceive me.

He does not perceive anything. He is still too happy savoring the afterglow of his good warm bath. His little libidinal pleasures. "It always takes him a few minutes to get back to normal after a bath, Mr. Haberman," Mother says. "He loves it when I bathe him. The warm water, the sponge, the suds."

"And when you touch him, Mother?" I querry straight-faced.

Again she is caught off guard and smiles embarrassedly.

I register each word and reaction well. They will serve me in good stead later on. One never knows enough, I say to myself. That is a maxim of mine. (One of many).

The first sound I hear from Brodski is the familiar cat's cry I heard at the park in front of the Maine Monument and have not been able to forget. His mewing does not surprise me now. I respond to it by offering up my warmest smile and laying hands on him. After this gesture, Mother breaks free from her reticence and invites me to join her for coffee. I agree, making sure first to fondle her son once more. Mother places Brodski gently, ever so gently, in his bed. A sort of hospital bed cut to crib's size. And I notice his size. For the first time I take measure of him. He is diminutive. I could carry him with one arm. Despite the absence of limbs, I realize now I had expected more. But there isn't more. This shrunken and misshapen torso is all there is. Not much . . . but it will have to do. Of course one can never measure a man by his size. Never will this aphorism prove truer than with Brodski.

Over steaming hot coffee I tell Mrs. Rivera how I can help improve her financial situation. How she is entitled to SSI benefits to supplement her meager social security income, and also how I can help initiate an application for food stamps. "With SSI supplementing your income, Mother dear, and food stamps, you'll be more than able to pay your rent. You'll be able to live in absolute luxury."

Mother smiles gratefully. She clasps my hand. It is evident that she is a warm, loving person. A humanist from an earlier age. And I have won her trust. Despite any previous report from the hospital it is easy with these types. I have never lost one yet.

13

I turn my attention to another subject. My inquiries concern her son's room. If I can learn no more than this, this morning, my day will be complete. It is. Everything falls into place. It could not be better. In almost conspiratorial tones Mother tells me how they have worked out their own special system of communication. Not based on words, but smiles and mewing sounds and gestures. The language is one of contortion and dissonance. Each time Brodski contorts his face or smiles in his special way, the old lady knows what he is thinking. How he is reacting. He has a thousand faces, she says with maternal pride. Thus she was able to create his room. Piece by piece, trial and error, each tidbit, momento, brick in place, is really Brodski's by design. The result of an enigmatic smile or a mewing sound only she could decipher. "It wasn't easy," she says. "Sometimes he can become very difficult. He's . . . how you say . . . a perfectionist. Everything has to be exactly right, otherwise he won't permit it. He's definitely a tyrant, my little one." I smile as I think to myself: Were Pharoh's pyramids built so differently? If only I know this much about him, it is enough. For one day's work, it is enough.

"I must be going," I say. "I have many things to do. Besides, perhaps I have already overstayed my welcome," I add demurely, searching the old lady's gaze for a reaction. It is just as I expected. "No, no," she exclaims anxiously. "Please stay. Here, have another coffee and some cake."

"Oh, well, just one more peek at Brodski then." I tiptoe into his room. Why tiptoe? To show concern, of course. Brodski lies in bed, a quaint infantile pout on his lips, his eyes directed towards mine. Whether he can see me or not is a matter of conjecture. I walk toward the window and pull the shade. Sunlight infiltrates the room. Brodski lets out a soft purring sound. He smiles. He can . . . he can see me. Or was he just responding to the light? Food for thought, but a good place to take my departure. Either way I leave with a good impression. The old lady will tell him of me if he doesn't already know.

14

Back at the office my Supervisor asks me about the pending case. What am I going to do with it? Accept or NA. (Not accept)? "Why, accept, of course, Mrs. Knox. Protective services. Both Mrs. Rivera and the cri du chat need all the help we can give them. Maybe later we'll put in a part-time Home Attendant. Right now the old woman's not ready for it. She'd never let a stranger come into her home. I think its enough for now if we just keep an eye on them."

Mrs. Knox and I have worked together for fifteen years, ever since I was first assigned to the Harlem Center. Not once has she called me by my first name. It is always "Mr. Haberman." I am, of course, no exception. She is that way with everyone. Her excessively formal approach is not that unusual at the Department. It blends in with the office decor. Anonymous, drab, impersonal, the same gray office furniture you find from Harlem to Wall Street. Sometimes when I speak to her I call her "Marilyn Knox" in an aggressively facetious tone. Not once in fifteen years have I ever called her just "Marilyn," though. Our mode of communication is as fixed and limited as Brodski's. Maybe more so, I think. Maybe more so.

While scribbling these notes about my Supervisor I am reminded of an incident that happened some thirty-three years ago. I had just graduated from college and started working for the Department at a downtown office. Even then, after only a few months on the job, I knew I hated it. And every day if I could manage it I would rush to the field. I thought I had someplace to go in those days. Youth always has someplace to go—even if it's only to dream. I even had some vague notion of getting involved in one way or another with the arts. As luck would have it, Mr. Burke, a civil service lifer, was returning to the office from lunch at the exact moment I was making my exit. And we bumped into each other accidently—he coming in, I going out of the elevator. Some words were exchanged, leading to more words. And then, I shall never forget his face—a

15

strange mixture of undisguised contempt, hostility and irony—when he said, "If you're not out of here by thirty, you'll never get out. You're stuck here all your life."

"That will never happen to me," I parried smartly.

"You want to bet?" came his quick retort.

"I'll bet my life on it," I said just as quickly.

When I reached forty,—I not only remembered the wager I had made, I realized I had lost it.

FORTY YEARS OLD! The year of my turnaround. What was I like at forty? I can hardly recall.

I think the most important thing about me then was that all the normal human responses had left me. Friendship, for example, held no further promise. I had gone as far as I could with it. There were only so many conversations one could have in a lifetime, and I had had them all. Intellect, too, I had stretched to its limits. I knew how far it had taken me. Not very. Work—I won't go into that now. And love. Ahh yes, L-O-V-E. And all its accoutrements . . . Passion, lust, sex . . . that alone could save me. Hardly. I had been there once, but now it was nothing more than a diversion, ah exercise. No, not even that. More like a repeat performance. One I had tired of and bought my last ticket for long ago. Whenever I pictured two people making love (and that was rare), it always struck me as something strange. It reminded me of one of those modern metallic sculptures with pieces scrambled together in interlocking fusion. But what brought people together in the first place? And what metallic paste or glue could hold them together and make them stick? . . . I didn't know.

People, in short, had nothing to offer me. I couldn't go anywhere without being vexed by them. If they came too close to me, I would virtually break out in a rash, and rather than scratch myself (which did no good anyway), I simply avoided them at every turn. Rush-hour crowds,

16

rallies, gatherings were anathema. Invariably I would take the rear seat in a bus (which I never rode during rush hour), or seat myself in the first row of an empty movie house on the extreme left. Even a blind man tapping his stick and waiting for help was enough to prompt me to make a stealthy retreat in the opposite direction. Not because I was against helping him, but rather because the very idea of getting so close to him was repugnant to me. Similarly with elevators. I would gallop like a madman or wait thirty minutes before sharing it with a fellow passenger.

And so, alone in my apartment, sitting, standing, pacing to and fro, eating chicken, drinking tea, walking to the corner and back at regular intervals, twice for newspapers, and three times or more merely to get out, pacing up and down the lobby corridor for the mailman who never delivered anything but bills to me, watching TV, listening to the radio, going to a movie, reading a book, waiting for the telephone which never rang, taking more tea, eating more chicken, waiting for the next news report, the next weather report, the next TV program, the next radio broadcast, scanning the movie clock for the next movie to be seen, searching my library shelves for the next book to be read even before I had finished the last one, I filled up every hour of every day of my life. All of it—the sitting, watching, listening, eating, reading, waiting—done without hope, without expectations, without the slightest delusion that anything would change. As my father had gotten into the habit of saying several years before his death, "life was just so much more chicken to eat every day."

Weekends were just as bad. After leaving work Friday at noon (and cashing my check at the bank every other week), I would march straight home and stay there till Saturday night. Then, more to break up the routine than to relieve the boredom, I would head over to a neighborhood tavern where I would remain until the murky dawn, when I would reel and stagger to my apartment to sleep. When I awoke on Sunday afternoon, I was already dreading Monday morning when I would have to return to work. Monday morning: only seventeen hours away.

And then something happend. No, *IT* happened! A small incident, seemingly meaningless, I almost can't remember it. But yes, it changed my life!

It had rained all week. The black asphalt gutters were slick and gleaming. There was a cleansing fragrance in the air. I was seated in an outside cafe in Greenwich Village. People, getting out for the first time all week, sat clustered in bunches before me. The nearest table, though more than several yards away, was still within hearing distance. As was my habit, I observed without being seen: Men and women, friends, groups of threes and fours and more; people speaking and telling each other what they must have said one thousand times before. My wife, my mistress, my girlfriend. My husband, my lover, my boyfriend. Do you know of a job for me? I'd give anything for a . . . How do you differentiate between love and sex? My mother has cancer of the bladder. Really? My father had a colestomy last month. I'm thirty years old. Do you believe it? I'm thirty years old! Why does it have to be this way? So you mean there's no answer!? People repeating the same conversations as if for the first time. Each time. The miracle of humanity: forgetfulness.

And all I could do was look, listen, spy and smell the air, so clean, the black asphalt gutters slick and gleaming. I asked myself what was strange about them. Different from myself. Was it the way they looked? But they all looked the same. We all looked the same. Except for our piecemeal features, there was no difference. It was the way they were *together*. The way they spoke, forgetting themselves in conversation. I had never talked like that. *They were leaping out of themselves and landing on the other shore.* I had never taken that leap. Never landed on the other shore. Gulping down a vodka tonic, I called a young waiter over. He possessed a naive innocence mixed with insatiable hunger. From an earlier talk I had ascertained that he was an actor. From out of town. In the big city to make good. He was looking forward to the day he would become eligible for unemployment benefits and be able to devote himself full time to making the audition rounds. Now, hardly knowing why, I told him I was a producer and he was right for a part in a play I was currently developing for Broadway. His eyes opened wide. The charm of youth, the gaiety, the smile, oh, what a smile, he could captivate anybody with that smile—or so he thought. Putting on my most impressive air, I continued, "You couldn't be better. The more I look at you and hear you speak, the more certain I am. And to think, meeting you like this. Purely by chance. It must be fate. Now, let's see. Today is Friday. I'll be out of town for the weekend. Call me Monday morning. Here, take my card. Opps, forgot it. Do you have something to write on? Don't forget now . . . Monday, 9:00 a.m. sharp. By the way, what did you say your name was?"

When I arrived Monday morning at the office the phone was already ringing. It was him. Not mincing words, I told him there must be a mistake, that he had dialed the wrong number, that this was the Welfare Center, not some theatrical producer's office. Sensing that he was about to hang up, I said, "Don't be so quick to go. From what I know of you actors, you might need public assistance more than you need any starryeyed audition. They always pan out badly anyway. Especially if you're not eligible for unemployment benefits."

Again: "No. I told you already. This is a Welfare Center."

He called back four times. Each time there was a little more dissappointment in his voice . . . except on the last call. When I answered the last call, all I heard was a lingering silence, followed by a clicking.

I KNEW I HAD FOUND MY WAY!!!

One month later, when by coincidence I came upon him again, this time waiting on tables at a different restaurant, I asked him, "What happened? Why didn't you call? . . .

19

You did? You must have taken down the wrong number. What a shame. We cast the part yesterday. But . . . but you really were perfect."

After walking several blocks on my way to the bus this morning I noticed an elderly couple smiling at me. Looking down, I discovered my fly was open. I wondered why the man at least hadn't stopped to tell me. My momentary rage at the passengers in the front of the bus who wouldn't make way for me was dispelled when I realized that I had not been the slightest bit embarrassed.

It is time for reflection, to call back the troops, to reconnoiter. First impressions are important but not everything. Mostly they are terribly deceiving. We bring ourselves into them without half-realizing it. But that is not my problem. I never bring myself into anything. Besides, I am not a moralist. One quick look and here's what's wrong. Nor am I a charlatan selling saran-wrapped panaceas to the world. I have no easy answers. Snap judgements are not part of my repertory. Many a medical man has lost his patient with just such a premature diagnosis. But not I. I never lose a patient once I set my sights on him. They are too few and far between to treat so shabbily. That would be immoral. If anything, my examinations are thorough, my labratory spotless. Perhaps I am a moralist.

This is what I have decided: I will send Mrs. Rivera a form letter advising her we have acceped Brodski's case. She will receive it tomorrow, or at the latest Wednesday. In the meantime I won't call her. Or visit.

No braggadocio intended but I have an absolute genius for w-a-i-t-i-n-g.

I was seated in a coffee shop in the Lincoln Center area this Sunday having brunch. Pancakes molten with butter and syrup and a generous portion of fruit salad on top. Four black people were sitting at the table to my left. The waitress passed a comment about one of the black people's weight when she surmised on the basis of the order that he was on a diet. The man and his three friends—another man and two women—all laughed uproariously. Evidently the waitress had hit on a sore spot of the dieting man. One of the women asked the waitress for her name. "Eloise," she answered, still bubbling over with laughter. And then a strange thing happened. All four blacks promptly introduced themselves. "Willis, James, Edna, Martha." They were so happy to enter . . . "human relations."

Are you so childlike, my darling?

Do you, too, crave Big Daddy?

Of course, the blacks weren't young. With young people today it is a whole different matter. But Brodski, considering his condition, is *OLD* at twenty-four.

Hallelujah! Mother called. Round one is mine. The most important round. It sets the tone for all the rounds to follow.

"When will we see you?" she said.

"Soon, Mother dear, soon."

She called at 3:30 in the afternoon. I was there at four. I had a choice. To respond or not to. I decided to respond at once.

I responded this way for several reasons:

First, I could hardly restrain myself any longer. It was Thursday already. And I am only human.

Second, I thought I detected an urgency in her voice. She made mention of Brodski being upset, possibly even ill. Could it have been my visit? Did he sense something? I don't know but I must find out.

21

Besides, last time, I disappointed her by leaving too soon. This time I shall make her happy by arriving before I'm expected. This way I keep my advantage. She (or he) beckons and I appear.

Of course, next time might be different. And there will be plenty of "next times."

Third, and most important, I bear glad tidings. A little gift. It is my way of finding out what I need to know. My special Rorschach test. I deliberated long and hard on what it should be. Finally I came upon just the right item. I am good at such things. Like all expert psychologists, I design my projective tests to catch my subjects off guard.

My little shopping spree was not without difficulties. I couldn't purchase my present ready-made at a store. I had to improvise. I had to purchase a costly art book first and cut out the print reproduction I wanted and then have it enlarged to poster size. After that was accomplished, I had it framed, a plain silver boarder, (quite expensive), and finally I had it gift wrapped. So much trouble for my little one. If only he knew: he is no trouble at all.

You should have seen his reaction. And it was genuine. I'm sure of that. Or should I say I made sure? Not only does this psychologist have his inkblots, but he has his placebo as well. Such things are mandatory in my work. Before giving Brodski his gift, I opened the other. Though it wasn't actually for him, at the time he couldn't know that. Mrs. Regina Douglas, our medical social worker, advised me what to get. She said a person suffering from his condition, a cri du chat, would most likely be attracted to the same things as an infant. Something glittering and shiny, preferably an object that moves. I purchased a shiny new egg beater for Mrs. Rivera. And waved it in front of her eyes. The old lady was absolutely gaga at my kindness. But Brodski wasn't. He showed no response. His eyes were dead. Then I unwrapped his present. A framed poster-size print of Edvard Munch's The Scream. Within seconds his face lit up. His eyes opened wide. So wide he looked ridiculous. It was as if at this moment he

22

was seeing the whole world. The room absolutely re-sounded with mewing sounds. He passed his test with flying colors.

Even Mrs. Rivera was impressed. "I have never see him respond like that," she said.

To this woman I am fast becoming a benefactor. To Brodski, a philanthropist of the arts. And really, I have no interest in the arts. In anything, "make-believe." Of all the riddles in the world, man's need for beauty baffles me most. But then, why has it perserved so long? Longer and more durable than governments, dynasties, moralities, civ-ilizations, even religions.

Could I be wrong?

No. Never!

I have one more little thing to do. My investment, if I calculate correctly, shouldn't cost me more than a few minutes. It's my way of following up the previous day's work. Like any good researcher, I have to validate my findings.

I visited them on Friday at noon. Almost at once my investment showed a handsome dividend. Mother was feeding her child. Brodski was slurping his food—soft-boiled eggs, the yellow ooze dribbling like a melting icicle from cheek to chin. He was refusing to take another swal-low when she uttered, half to herself, "He has no appetite."

I replied quite harmlessly, "What does he live on, air?"

She looked at me with solemnity and sadness, her voice giving vent to the most ancient of maternal grievances. "Not air, Mr. Haberman, but that." And she pointed to his room filled with paintings, various art objects and an old RCA windup victrola.

Immediately the blood began to course madly through my veins. I stood up from my chair and headed for the door. My last words before leaving their humble abode were, "Bon appetite."

SO BRODSKI'S AN AESTHETE! A lover of beauty. Well, well, it is just as I have surmised all along. My little ugly duckling is really a swan.

All right, little one, we shall travel to Parnassus together. On Mt. Olympus you will stand and see the Seven Wonders of the World. Did I say you will stand? My error. I will stand and upon my shoulders you will see. Just as Atlas bore the weight of the world on his shoulders, I shall bear you on mine . . . To see.

An aesthete? Yes: I have found my Road to Damascus.

From now on I pledge all my time to Brodski. Is he worthy of it? That is entirely up to me. Social Counselors tell us that we get from a relationship what we put into it. I shall put myself into Brodski. For sheer effort and single-mindedness of purpose, no one shall ever have given more.

Over the next several weeks not a day goes by that I don't visit Brodski. Always I bring him gifts. Not necessarily those you can purchase in a store. One day I might adjust a painting that is hanging lopsided or is off center by a fraction, another day I might tilt his head to make it a trifle easier for him to observe his marvelous view. All in all the household begins to take on a different feel. My own.

My greatest gift, however, is that I offer Brodski what he cannot receive from anyone else. A mirror to see himself in. Not what he looks like, but what he is like. In every one of my acts, gestures, smiles, faces, there is only one motive. To make his room, his world, his sanctuary a little more beautiful. To make the outside correspond to what is within.

For the first day and part of the second, Brodski wouldn't let me enter his room. Mother had to stay as chaperon until I won his trust. I did not take offense at this slight. On the contrary, I would have been disappointed if he had acted otherwise. After all, what else does the little fellow have but this? For him, to as much as twitch a muscle

24

requires a prodigious effort. He lies on one side of his torso, then, thanks to Mother's gentle nudging, he lies on the other. This room is more than his home. It is his temple, his shrine. A place for him to pray. It comprises all he has and what he is. Thus I gather all my forces. It is the first place I invade.

The thought occurs to me that in all of Brodski's household there is not the smallest space for a game room. I must make one. Indoor sports in the usual sense are not my forte. Sex has never been my game. Whatever modicum of interest I had waned years ago. But there are other indoor sports far more interesting than sex. And one doesn't even have to work up a sweat to play.

For the past few days Brodski has not taken his eyes off me when I visit. Each time I move, I bring a ray of beauty into his home. If I have not created the apartment, I have certainly brought out its best features. Thanks to me, his world finally receives the attention it deserves. It is not that I have impeccable taste or am so gifted a decorator. It is just that I know how much he needs *BEAUTY*. It is my job to accomodate myself to his need. Like a good curator who enhances the paintings in his museum by ensuring their proper placement and location, I enhance the *objets d'art* in Brodski's room. To begin with, his prints are brought into line. If I can help it, they are never off by so much as a fraction of an inch. The light, thanks to my chiarascuro lighting, shines on them perfectly. At any time of day he can see each to best advantage. Of course, I don't teach Mother the workings of the dimmer lighting system I have installed. Thus when evening comes, by the very loss of beauty, he knows I'm not there. Brodski's tiny sculptured pieces and figurines are also arranged to best advantage. In the way they face each other, where they stand, on what dresser, night table, desk, each becomes in its own way a singular work of art.

25

My efforts are not limited to Brodski's room, I also make my talents felt in Mother's. Why not? Beauty knows no limits. Why should Brodski's world be restricted to one room? My efforts do not go unappreciated by Mother. Though she doesn't fully comprehend why I am doing what I am doing, she approves wholeheartedly. She can see the improvement, maybe not in the aesthetic sense, but more importantly, in the way her son responds. The hideous smoked mirrors (Brodski could never bear to look at himself) go first. Next, the plastic covers. Then the horrid photos of the Kennedys and King. (She argued here, I admit). And also, those absurdly grotesque religious articles and savings. (She argued here, also). With a little effort, hiding one thing, accentuating another, even the most unattractive women can be made attractive. There is no such thing as an ugly woman. I am fast coming to the opinion that there is no such thing as a tasteless room.

Without doubt all those hours I wracked my brains studying lighting techniques were not in vain. The way Brodski never closes his eyes lately tells me that. On earlier visits I noticed that whenever he was exposed to the unsightliness of Mother's room, he would go into that vegetal stare of his. Now he doesn't.

So now he has two rooms. Thanks to me, his world has grown twice as large.

Does Brodski appreciate me? Let us see. One day I remove the shade from his lamp and insert two five-hundred-watt bulbs. The strongest voltage possible for that particular lamp. With the bare bulbs shining on the off-white walls, the room is illuminated to such an extent that the infamous cat's cry not heard in recent days now reappears, reaching startling crescendoes. I respond by lowering the lights, dimming them just a little, not enough. Brodski continues to wail. I continue to dim the lights, knowingly passing the point where his cries or lack of same tells me to stop. He does not understand. He has built up such confidence in me. Hard won confidence. I continue to diminish the light to the point where I doubt he can see

26

his precious prints, much less appreciate them. I watch the little darling closely as he strains his eyes. He lets out a shriek for help, but Mother is out and only I am here. Only I can resolve his plight. He cannot comprehend why I am so off in my aesthetic judgement. My taste before has always proved impeccable. At last I pass him a befuddled look. What do you want of me? it says. Finally, just at the moment when insight occurs, "Aha!" I shout. I transpose the bulb, put on the lamp shade, and all is well. Poor darling, what a time he had of it. And you ask: Does he appreciate me?

Of course, I want to be much more than merely appreciated. To this end I have devised a game. A game in which the participant cannot lose. It is simple enough. One needs only a theatrical spotlight, a tray, a stopwatch, a picture that has some special value to one participant, and a dozen or so other art objects, so differing in quality and aesthetic worth from one to another that their variance can be perceived by any fairly refined eye.

Brodski has such an eye. He also has a favored picture (his poster print of Munch's The Scream). Therefore I had only to provide a spotlight, a stopwatch, a tray, and several dozen objects possessing varying degrees of aesthetic worth. Though some of the materials for my games are quite costly, I have accumulated quite a tardy contingency fund for just such purposes. The country spends billions on its pleasures; should I quibble about the cost of mine. If anything, I am a man of the times. Now to the game:

I focus the spotlight on Brodski's favorite painting. With a click from the extension cord switcher I can illuminate the print any time I want. Then I place the aesthetic objects in a tray upon the dresser directly in front of Brodski's bed. Two at a time. He could not see them more clearly; he does not even have to crane his neck (if he had a neck) an inch. His task is to differentiate between each pair, to select the more prepossessingly beautiful object. He can accomplish this easily; a purr, a nod or a smile is all that is needed. Each time he does so I reward him by putting the spotlight on Munch's The Scream. Depending upon the time it takes him to decide and the difficulty of the choice, his favorite picture will remain center stage. Since I learn quickly that Brodski can hold his gaze unstintingly for long stretches of time, I vary my reward anywhere from 10 seconds to perhaps as much as a minute or two. Because of the way I have constructed the game and his infallible eye, his reward has been cut short to 10 seconds only once. And in all honesty that was due to no failing of his, but rather of mine. Once, purely by accident, I miscalculated. Perhaps it wasn't an accident. The fact that without exception Brodski had been selecting the correct object instantaneously (not once did I even have a chance to use my stopwatch) might have had something to do with it.

In any event, in all future games resembling this one, the gradient scale of difference between one object and another will be less. A great deal less.

ASSHOLES!!! They want to take Brodski away from me. Before I've even started. Before I've even insinuated myself in his soul. Some fool comedian from downtown came up with the bright idea of calling for a realignment in the East Harlem area: Procedure 2-387. Effective immediately. We are to transfer all cases north of 116th street to Units F through K.

I rush to my Supervisor's desk. Mrs. Knox bids me wait. "Can't you see I'm busy talking to Mrs. Sampson, Mr. Haberman? Please wait your turn." Mrs. Knox is absolutely religious about office protocol. She knows every procedure and memorandum by heart. She follows every regulation to the letter. Procedure 3-679 says this; Memorandum 5-354 says that. In the afternoons, when the office empties out, she keeps herself busy by studying procedures and memorandums over and over until she has them memorized like some apple-a-day schoolgirl in Sunday school class. "I'm sorry, Mr. Haberman," she says, "but no matter what you say, it's still against departmental policy. We can't allow it. It's procedure!"

"But my client will die without me as his caseworker, Mrs. Knox. I speak to Mrs. Rivera at least once a day. Often more. It's a special case. A special situation. I've only had this case for a short time now, but already I've made fantastic progress. If you let me, I can perform miracles with this client."

"Well, then, Mr. Haberman, you'll just have to perform miracles on some other client."

"But Brodski's used to me. And besides, Mrs. Rivera won't let anyone else in the apartment but me. Mrs. Knox, I'll even keep this case if you don't give me credit for it. You don't have to count it on my caseload. That's right. You heard me. My caseload will be one case larger than anyone else's in our unit."

This last comment registers. Parity is the law of the land in civil service. No caseworker in Unit B, in the entire Department, does anything without getting credit for it. Statistics keep everybody doing the same job . . . statistically. Everybody is insured the same amount of work . . . statistically. No more can a conscientious caseworker ask. Two (2) pending cases per worker a week; one hundred (100) cases per worker in all. Not one iota more or different from the rest. The civil service snail marches on in perpetuity.

Mrs. Knox's reaction is one of great puzzlement. In fifteen (15) years she has not heard me say anything so strange. I can hear her civil servant's computer clickety click: What could he be up to? Is this an easy case for him? Probably doesn't even have to visit. Must have worked out some sort of system with the client to make it easy on himself. Despite our fifteen years together in Harlem, Mrs. Knox doesn't know me at all.

Suddenly the computer flashes into synch.

"My, my, Mr. Haberman, you really feel strongly about this case."

"And it's only an inter-office transfer, Mrs. Knox. We aren't even being asked to transfer the cases to another center or downtown to C.O." (Central office).

"I'm sorry, Mr. Haberman, but no matter how extenuating you say the circumstances are, this has to be my final decision. Not mine, you understand . . . but Procedure 2-387."

I take a chance. Overstepping Mrs. Knox, and bypassing all that's holy in office hierarchy, I head straight for the Director's office. Tom Sanders, born black but truly green, a plant lover par excellence, holds that estimable position. His office rivals the Botanical Gardens. On every ledge and border, in every nook and cranny, corner and crevice, his green thumb has given birth. Never between the hours of 9 and 5 p.m. can anyone disturb this man from his chaparral habitat. In past office visits I have learned more in an hour from Tom Sanders about plants and flowers than thirty-three years with the Department has ever taught me about casework. This time I don't even make an effort to wade through his jungle defenses. Rather I mention something about a hundred-year-old bonsai tree. His ears perk up. His green thumb stops watering a cabbage plant in midstream. A hundred year-old-bonsai tree is a real coup. Anything much older is a national treasure in Japan. And I know where to get it for him. After discussing terms—where, when, how much—I barter for my favor. "Despite the new procedure on transferring cases, Tom," I say, "there's a certain case I'd like to keep. You see . . ."

He interrupts me. "No time to discuss it now, Haberman. You've been here long enough. Do what you think best."

"But Mrs. Knox . . ."

"Never mind Mrs. Knox. I'm the Director of this center, am I not? Now when did you say you can get me that bonsai . . ."

Even before I close the door behind me I can hear the familiar water spray jet out from his plant jug. And seconds later, if I strain my ears hard enough, I can also hear him on the phone with Mrs. Knox. "Now what kind of new procedure was that caseworker talking about?"

As I return to my desk, I notice Mrs. Knox's eyes averting mine. All her attention is seemingly focused on a case record she is reading. I think: Yes, Mrs. Knox, what the hell kind of procedure were you talking about!"

I just realized that up to this point, I've neglected to comment on my fellow workers other than my Director and my Supervisor, Mrs. Knox. Those worthies who make up Unit B. That's what we're called here. I'm B-24. Someone else is B-23; B-22; B-21. And so here follows Unit B:

To begin with, there's Richard Gould, B-23. Married, two children, smokes a pipe, and lately reads a lot. Hates this job but states he would hate any other job even more. Richard Gould would never put himself in a position where he could fail. Be threatened. Have to compete. For that reason he is important to me. Except for his habit of flinging the phone at me on occasion, I find I can bully him all I want to with small fear of retaliation. And I do. Oh, he has all the defenses: the entire gamut from indifference to moral lethargy. "What's the difference anyway" is his daily recitativo. But underneath. What denial. What self-betrayal. He can't fool me. Every now and then when I need a whipping boy, he's perfect. Of course I try not to take undo advantage of him. That would be unfair and tantamount to self-destruction. For if I did, I couldn't stretch out my good fortune. Besides, I would never give myself away. If you know that about me, you know a lot. Have I said that before? Even if I have, it's worth repeating: I never give myself away.

Then there's John P. Nolan, B-22. Rodent Face, thirtyish, and a devout Catholic. Once studied for the priesthood. He missed his calling. He should have stayed there. He's a born saint. Martyrdom as pure as his (he volunteers daily to make my field visits; those of others in the unit, too) I find laughable. To give you an indication of the laughability of his condition, he admires Mr. Gould. I quote: *He's made a contribution. He's got a wife and kids. I don't have that. They're part of him. I think that's wonderful. If I didn't love anyone.* . . his squeaky mouse voice fades here before continuing . . . *If I die I won't have anyone to remember me.* I ask you. Who can top that? Is it any wonder the Pope is

31

against the pill? With devotees like Rodent Face around, what smart politician wouldn't want to increase the electorate? And if anything, the Church is political. As if you didn't know.

Next follows B-21: Arlene Sampson. A black woman fifty-five years of age with an ego grounded in Mother Earth. And she is Mother Earth. Not a day goes by that I don't hear "Big Daddy" (her husband) and "Mother" (her mother) and "the kids" (her children) pass from her lips. After working all day at the office she goes home to cook for the entire family. But especially "Big Daddy." When she returns to the office the next morning she always has something "bad" to say about him. How unappreciative he is. How cheap. How he's always complaining about something. How he's never satisfied. "The kids" are eighteen-year old Darcie (her "baby") and twenty-four-year-old Donnie (her "big boy"). They call her at the office once a day, every day, to receive instructions on how to live their lives. To be so connected to the world, to know your place so well, to have a place . . . it is any wonder I need Brodski?

The games continue:

As I have been doing pretty much right along, I continue to make it easy for Brodski. The more I indulge him today, the harder it will be for him tomorrow. I remember as a child wanting to sleep late in the morning and my father coming into my room and cruelly awakening me. "Wake up . . . get out of bed." I have never forgotten my mother's reaction on one special occasion. "Let him sleep, Abe, he'll have to get up early the rest of his life, now for school, and later for work."

So I allow Brodski to sleep late. He, too, will have to rise early the rest of his life. And like my father, I will be the one to wake him.

This afternoon, unbeknownst to Brodski, I place a miniature portable radio on his window ledge. Disco sounds blare away in his room. Brodski's wince is my command. Immediately I speed into action. First I shut the window, slipping the radio behind my back and into my right rear pocket. Next, in easy sight of Brodski's hawking eye, I hurry to his RCA windup victrola. Seconds later the soothing strains of a Haydn concerto stretch languidly across his room. Brodski's purr tells me I am right. His taste is classical. His smile thanks me for transporting him to a calmer age.

Upon entering Mt. Sinai Hospital a little past noontime today on my way to a pending case, I noticed a group of children congregated around a telephone booth in the lobby. One little boy looked like me when I was his age. He'll look like me when he's my age. What will I look like . . . then? Supressing an anxious feeling in the pit of my stomach, I decided not to make the visit and rushed over to Brodski instead.

Not all my games require so much of me. Sometimes (far too rarely) my best ideas come from completely unexpected sources. It is just a matter of keeping one's eyes and ears open. Just as a lover sees all the world's objects as treasure for his beloved, I see everything for Brodski.

For the past several weeks there has been a recurring problem in the Brodski household. A newly arrived tenant is the cause. It is this denizen's habit to fill his skull each morning, noon and night with the same disco sounds. Closing the windows is not a real defense against these mind-obliterating waves of sound. Neither is turning up Brodski's RCA victrola. Even if it were possible to increase the decibels of this ancient machine, which it isn't, it would do little good as Brodski's own music would only have to compete against his neighbor's hi-fi. The sonorant sounds of the cry of the cat have been on the increase ever since the disco-loving neighbor moved in.

But I have solved the problem. What I did was really quite simple. It only required a pair of headphones and a tape player. When I placed the headphones around Brodski's head, permitting him for the first time in what must have seemed like forever to hear his precious music undisturbed, his eyes shone with such an eerie glitter that it gave me chills. There was no telling where he was transported this time. But I know one thing: he was no longer with us. It is quite conceivable that whereever he was, he learned the meaning of the expression: I GIVE THANKS TO THE GODS. Yes: I am fast becoming a God to Brodski. A God that doesn't even ask for thanks.

What I said a few pages back about art deserves further comment. I ask myself why, if I feel the way I do, do I allow art to take up such a large sphere of my life? Certainly Brodski is not the first beauty-lover I have chosen to play my games with.

Am I nothing more than a Freudian footnote repelled by the very thing I love?

Love Brodski? No. Never!

I've gotten in the habit of visiting Brodski every morning. Or rather I make it my business to visit him. I want the little fellow to start the day off right. Mother has told me more than once how Brodski always has trouble with his breakfast. "He can't hold a mouthful," she says, "or if he does, he'll hold it for hours at a time without swallowing. He'll get sick if he don't eat, Mr. Haberman," she bellows in panic. "He'll die. He's so stubborn . . ."

I have found a way to whet Brodski's appetite. Every morning I bring him something that makes his tiny bird's mouth water. Not caviar or chocolate mousse. Not even that wholesome and nutritious baby formula I have taken the pains to persuade Ms. Gonzalez, assistant to the Chief Nutritionist at Mt. Sinai Hospital, to make up for him specially. That goodie I've presented to Mrs. Rivera already. What I bring now is for Brodski alone. I bring him BEAUTY. One day it might be a tray emblazoned with a Modigliani face; another day a saucer or cup with a Picasso or Matisse imprint. Each morning I visit he eats his special baby formula to the accompaniment of the soothing strands of Haydn or, for variation, Chopin, the headphones I gave him enveloping his little head. I place my art-treasure before him, and only when he swallows his mouthfuls like a good little child does Daddy give him his reward.

For the rest of the morning I can rest secure. Breakfast is the most important meal of the day and I know my darling has had his. It shall hold him in good stead until I return later for lunch. Indeed, he can't wait for my return. I can just hear his little tummy churning with anticipation. And why not? Is there another parent in all the world who feeds his babe quite like me?

This daily breakfast visit is accomplished not before clocking in at the Center, but after. Generally, I'm clocked in by 8:00 a.m. and on my way to Brodski's only minutes later. Luckily for me, Brodski resides only a few short blocks from the office. When I return to the office late, my time card covers me. Regardless of how my time card reads, though, and despite the fact that I deliver the Daily News to Mrs. Knox's bin religiously every morning before I take off for Brodski's—once, when all the usual newspaper stands were closed because of a crushing snowstorm, I walked eighteen blocks out of my way to assure such delivery—Mrs. Knox still applies her rules mercilessly. If I'm not sitting at my desk at precisely 9:00 a.m. ready for work, I'm late.

"Where have you been, Mr. Haberman? On a coffee break already?"

"No, Mrs. Knox," I improvise, "to the field. I've even posted it on my W712." (Field record form).

(I would if she'd let me).

(She doesn't).

35

"Mr. Haberman, you know very well workers aren't allowed to go to the field anymore directly from their homes. Clearly Memorandum 6-873 forbids that *clearly*. Workers first have to clock in at the office. And then, only if it's an emergency, and they obtain special permission from their Supervisor, can they leave for the field. But *never* under any circumstances before 9:15 a.m. Mr. Haberman, Memorandum 6-873 has been in effect for nearly two years now."

"But . . ."

"There are no buts about it, Mr. Haberman. From now on you'll either be seated at your desk promptly at 9:00 a.m. like your co-workers, or else I'll have to report you to your Director."

Mrs. Knox's eyes rise above mine and search out the other workers.

"Oh, by the way, Unit B, thanks to Mr. Haberman, I'm going to have to keep a time sheet on my desk for you to sign in on every morning. No, Mr. Nolan, it's not enough that you clock in officially downstairs. I have to know who's doing an honest day's work around here and who's not."

"Why? Because your Supervisor says so, that's why!"

NOTE TO MYSELF

From here on, Brodski's daily morning breakfast visits will be made one half hour earlier. He *must finish* his breakfast by 8:45 a.m.

Mrs. Knox and the other workers notice other changes about me. Most evident is my new found panache. Every day now I come into the Center dressed to the hilt. Accustomed to my pre-Brodski days of disheveled bachelorhood, they must now see me as something of a dandy.

In my entire workaday life no one in the Department has ever seen me so made up. "Could he have a lady friend?" says John P. Nolan. "No, never," comes the quick retort from Mother Earth. "Everyone knows Haberman's attitude toward women. He hates them."

"If so, she must really be some dish," continues Rodent Face, "to get old Haberman dressed up and polished like this. He looks like a veritable peacock the way he's preened. What's that: pomade on his hair? He even smells pretty."

Mother Earth, who combines with her absolute certainty an amnesiac's memory bank, hones in on who.

"I bet it's someone in the office," she says. "Or at least up here in Harlem. Why else would he dress this way unless he was going to be with her every day?"

"Or could it be a client?" querries Richard Gould, our guilt-laden jew, who always thinks (and says) the worst.

Every day is a maddening rush to get out of the office. I do eight hours' work in three. Exhausted but exhilarated after I finish my paper work, I'm ready to leave for the field. No, not for the field . . . for Brodski.

My fellow workers stare at me in narrow-eyed hate. Why do I rush so? How do I get my work done so quickly? It's been established that I don't have a female friend.

"At this rate he'll do a full month's work in a week," complains Mother Earth to Rodent Face.

The look on Rodent Face is the same look every fledgling priest must have the first time a member of his flock asks the great question.

One morning Mrs. Knox calls me to her desk for a conference. Her face wears an expression I've seen only once before in fifteen years. That was the time someone in the office stole her binful of memos and procedures. Since then she padlocks her desk cell. "It will never happen again!" she shrieked in hysterical frenzy. Though she never actually accused me of the crime, it was evident from the way she acted towards me for the next several months that she held me to blame.

Now she has the same expression on her face. "Mr. Haberman," she says, "your W712 is highly irregular this month. It seems you've posted ten visits on your Brodski case in addition to the basic statutory visit. Mr. Haberman, it's impossible for you to spend so much time with one client and not do a disservice to all your others. If you continue this way, you'll neglect your entire caseload."

"But Mrs. Knox," I interrupt, "that's not true. Just look at my case record on Brodski. Every visit was necessary, and I've visited all my other cases due this month too."

"Please don't interrupt me till I'm finished, Mr. Haberman. I've already read your case records. We both know a worker can enter anything he wants to in his case record entries. I'm talking *statistics*. Downtown doesn't come here or call us and ask how many clients did you help at the end of the month. Do this or do that. No. They just want us to keep our controls up to date. My job has turned me into a statistical clerk. That's all any of us really are, Mr. Haberman. But with one big difference. I'm the one that has to make out the monthly reports that go downtown. Now tell me, how am I going to explain these numbers? Tell them you visit ninety-nine cases once every three months for ten minutes each, and another for four weeks straight without a letup? Mr. Haberman, it's downtown who won't stand for it. Not me. If it were up to me, you could enter anything you want to in your case records. I wouldn't even read them." She pauses here, pawing the ground before the kill. "Now, Mr. Haberman, as I was saying, if you don't change your work habits regarding this case, I'm going to have to transfer it to another worker like it should have been transferred in the first place."

From that day on I don't post one visit more than I'm statistically allotted on my W712 for case SSI 6718798 aka Brodski.

Moreover, I furnish newspaper delivery service to my Supervisor every morning free of charge.

"Oh, keep your money, Mrs. Knox. It's on me!"

38

The way they spoke about it in the office this morning.
On the trains. In the streets. Tears trickling down their
silly faces. Their voices cracked with pain. Why would
anyone want to kill him? An artist. A music maker. A pure
soul like him. The killer must be crazed ! Sick! Nuts! Why?
Why? Why? They're so dumb. So blind. I wanted to tell
them why. Everything inside me ached to tell them why.
But I didn't. Why should I? They wouldn't understand
anyway. They dare not understand. They're happy to live
their lives through other people. They know everything
there is to know about other people. Celebrities: This one
and that one. Where he was born. When she died. When
they were married. Divorced. Who she's having an affair
with. Had an affair with. Where she had her children.
When. And with whom. Her abortion. Abortions. They
have a celebrity-scrapbook programmed in their minds
indelibly recording their favorite's first hit. First success.
First break. First! First! First! When was my first break?
When does my career start? Change? Turn? Never. That's
when. That's why he was killed. Because HE HAD CELEB-
RITY! Because HE DID SUCCEED! Because HE IS A
HOUSEHOLD NAME! Why him? Why not me? Why
should he have everything and me nothing? Why should I
have to be here every day doing a job I detest; in my room
alone every night watching his ugly face on TV; listening
to his songs on the radio? They're not my songs. It's not me
gaining acclaim. He told us lies. All artists tell us lies. Turn
our heads from the truth. From reality and experience.
Our Experience! All artists would have us believe that everything is possible. Sure. For him it was possible. He made it!
But what about me?! Who's knocking my door down?
Where's my chauffeur-driven limosine? When was the last
time I received the plaudits of the crowd? A standing

39

ovation? A single compliment? If I died today, who would care? I hate all artists. I hate anyone who wants to be different. Exceptional. I hate anyone who wants special attention. Who gets preferential treatment. I hate anyone who tries to ensnare us in his net of artistic grandiosity. Who does and makes and creates and gives birth to. Who aspires to become more than he is. I hate anyone who believes in life! It's not true. They're not alive. They're all fixed, immutable, dead inside. This office and that chair and these case records on my desk and the four walls in my apartment and chicken dinner every night. That's it! Once and for all! For a lifetime!

I'll tell you something. A little secret I've known ever since that first time in the Village with the actor. I'll tell you when we're not dead. When we do come to life. The killer knows. The one that did away with your music maker. He knows. That's why he murdered him. The moment he saw him lying there on the ground in a crumpled heap . . . he knew. Ask him. He'll tell you. Only when something is dead can we possess it. Only when it's dead can we really control it. Conquer it. Make it our own. Until then it's transient, free. It can come and go. Only when something is reduced to its final state; when we've made it a thing, an object, fleshlike and carnal, is it ours completely. That's when God must have known he was God. Not when he made the world but when he destroyed it. Massacred it. When he told us we were going to die. When he made us conscious of that. That's why he kills us in the end. He becomes immortal when we die. He lives forever only when we cease to be. If it were up to me, I'd exterminate all the artists in the world. All the believers. I tell you I'm glad. Glad I tell you . . . Glad . . .

NOTES TO MYSELF
Somehow I've managed to either lose or misplace (not like me) the detailed entries I've made on various games I've recently played with Brodski. Rather than attempt to recount them here, it is enough to say they proved extremely successful.

Brodski is progressing—if I may use the expression—by leaps and bounds.

NOTES TO MYSELF
The little fellow is getting oh so bold. He has delusions of grandeur. He thinks he can stand on his own two feet without me to support him. Good. Let him think so. When it is time for him to fall, the incline will be all the steeper. And he will FALL.

NOTES TO MYSELF
Things are going along much too smoothly. Beyond all expectations, progress is being made. I must put a slight halt on such proceedings. I don't want to spoil Brodski. Not true. I don't want to spoil myself.

I ask myself: If I had no arms and legs and my world consisted of no more than the smallest-size mattress of a hospital crib-bed, what would I want most in the world?

The answer: I know the answer.

41

All the signs are there. Brodski is ready for the next stage. Previously, when I visited him, if I was a bit tardy or off schedule for noonday lunch, he would become irritable or not touch a bite. Now, even if I don't join him, his appetite couldn't be better. I can remember when his gaze followed my every move. When I was the hub and center of his attention. But no longer. In fact, this afternoon when I appeared, he hardly raised his eyes. But don't get the idea that his indifference is repugnance. No. Quite the opposite. It is rather that I have become like a member of the family to him. As an old beat-up piece of furniture no one notices. These are the surest signs of love and trust I know. Of course this change didn't come all at once, but gradually, over a prolonged period of time. Naturally I had something to do with it.

Nor does he lose himself in my games as he once did. I have only to compare his earlier results (which, of course, I keep) to more recent findings to realize that his average mean time for staring at his favorite painting, Munch's The Scream, has lessened considerably. In the early days he could hold his gaze for hours at a time, once even achieving the impressive total of three and a half. Now the best he can manage, no matter what tricks of contrast and shading I employ, is a scant ten minutes. And his intensity is gone. No longer does he whine and shriek if I take the print away, or illuminate it poorly, or even as I did in one special instance, deny it to him altogether. Indeed, as with everything else in this four-walled enclosure, (if I might paraphrase) he has grown accustomed to its face. This is as good a barometer as there is that he has outgrown our first phase and is ready for the second.

Of course, as I intimated earlier, none of these changes

merely happened by themselves. They needed a helping hand. But my fingers have always been long and dextrous; "piano fingers," my mother called them. Thus for a period spanning several weeks now I have exhibited no real talent for creating games worthy of inspiring his attention. They are all pale imitations of what used to be, lacking in originality and power—and what is more crucial here, far too similar and repetitive. It is only a tribute to Brodski's extraordinary aesthetic need that his interest did not completely wane long ago.

I have helped him reach this second stage in other ways too. For example, by propping his little head and torso against a pillow, I have made it possible for him to (in effect) sit at a window for hours at a time and gaze at his wonderful view. Even when I'm not there he can maintain this position and usually does. And once even, when Mother went shopping, I carried him to the rooftop so he was able to see the four-cornered vista of the city. If anything can inspire a man to spread his wings, I have always maintained, it is a lovely view. From the look on Brodski's face I'm not that far wrong. If he wasn't ready to fly, I daresay he did stretch his wings. Or at least those vestigial excrescenes we call as much.

And this is just what I want. This is the Second Phase. To stretch Brodski's wings. To prepare him to fly. No longer must he be content with or limited to the four-walled environ of his home. He must be allowed to reach whatever aesthetic heights he can. To achieve this, I will have to take him out into the world. He will have to see the world. Only then will he be able to grow in proportion to what he can absorb. This, then, is what I have been preparing Brodski for. To yearn for the world. To want to see, touch and feel the world. Yes: The world for Brodski will come into focus, but I will adjust the lens.

Damn it! Nothing comes easy! Nothing happens quite the way one expects it. Here I was indulging myself in idle thoughts on how well Brodski was progressing and what happens? A real problem occurs. Mrs. Rivera objects to my taking her son outdoors. Oh, I expected some of the usual arguments passed down from time immemorial by mothers protecting their children. In this case, more understandable than most. The world is crazy today. On every street corner and in every unguarded building lurks danger. People are tossing absolute strangers in front of subway cars. But she is more adamant than I could have imagined. I only need listen to her words and observe her face to know it will be no easy task to sway her. "Mr. Haberman," she exclaims, "that is the one thing I cannot allow. I did once but never again."

"You mean he's only been outside once in his entire life, Mother? Is that what you said?"

"Once, Mr. Haberman, and I shall never forgive myself for it. It was the day I had a doctor's appointment due to my arthritis and I had to leave him with my girlfriend. How was I to know she would take him out? I gave her strict instructions. Mr. Haberman, he saw something that day. Something happened to him that day. I don't know what, but I swore to myself I would never let it happen again."

"When? Where?" I query, already knowing the answer.

"It was at the Maine Monument, Mr. Haberman, last fall. No, it wasn't the children playing that annoyed him, or the odd looks he got. My friend insists it wasn't that at all. It was something far worse . . ." She pauses. "Only no one knows what."

"No one, Mother?" I say, feigning incredulity.

44

"No one, Mr. Haberman," she continues, shaking her head for emphasis. "For a whole week he couldn't eat. He just laid there like a corpse. Not a cry, not a sound out of him. The poor child. That's when I brought him to the hospital. And when he was discharged, the social worker there referred us to your agency. That's how we met you. Don't you remember?"

"But I never knew what caused his illness, Mother. I just took it for granted it had something to do with his general condition. Are you absolutely positive it doesn't? How can you be so certain about something like that? That it was something outside!?!

"Mr. Haberman," she answers, "ask me anything but don't ask me to let my little one go outside again. The world," she stammers, "the world is not a kind place for the likes of him." Her face turns deathly serious. "Mr. Haberman, he has absolutely nothing to defend himself with against the world."

The discussion goes on and on. I let her make all her points, hoping to hear a flaw in her argument, hoping to find something against which I can mount a counterattack. But nothing emerges. The only thing to my benefit is that Brodski, I notice, is listening too. Just look at his face. He knows what I want. He wants the same thing. The little darling is upset with Mother for preventing him from going outdoors. That is good. I will go home now and plan my counterattack. Brodski's last grimace has brought my beachhead into view.

NOTES TO MYSELF

One thing I must never do. I must never depart from my battle plan. I must never forsake what I know. No general likes to conquer a barren land. Better to fill it with the world's treasure. Only then does it become worthy of conquest. Only then does the enemy have something to lose. Any butcher at the slaughterhouse knows as much. . . . So I must fatten Brodski up with the world's treasure. There is no departing from that. In addition to Brodski, *Mother will have to lose.*

One day after Mother's affront I withdraw my services from the Brodski household. Days go by and I don't call or visit. Nor do I answer Mrs. Rivera's telephone calls. I have instructed my unit clerk and co-workers to inform Mrs. Rivera when she calls that I am too busy to talk, or in conference, or out in the field. My co-workers are only too happy to oblige. One of the Department's most trying problems is client telephone calls. Actually these calls serve as a kind of safety valve. Overtaxed, daily enraged by the monotony of their jobs, the caseworkers vent their frustrations on the clients. The clients can't fight back. They can hardly afford the telephone calls. Thus every time a telephone rings in the office the caller is bombarded by a series of barks, growls, and slam-downs. How do these good samaritans rationalize their behavior? They don't. Oh, there is always someone who has to be different. Mrs. Abigail Hill, for instance, better known as "Dear Abbie," daughter of a Baptist minister from the Deep South. She insists in her slow-minded drawl that it is for the client's own good. "They can become too dependent upon us caseworkers, you know. Why, if we let them, they'd call every day. More than once!"

It goes without saying that I am no exception to this Telephone Answering Rule. But, as with everything else, I've put my own stamp on it. A favorite ploy of mine involves "Spanish-speaking only" clients. When these leather-skinned Latinos call, such vituperation and curse words spew from my lips that sometimes it takes the better part of the morning to get it all out. And why not? Not only don't they fully realize that I'm cursing them, they can't report me, certainly not to—and this is critical—Mrs. Knox. What could they say? "No hablo ingles"; "No comprendo."

Come to think of it, ever since meeting Brodski my telephone etiquette has improved considerably. Well, as they say, for every winner there's a loser.

Mrs. Knox has proved pliant in solving this problem. As usual, she merely invokes her own set of rules. "From now on," she said one fine morning, "Group B will not accept telephone calls from clients after noontime unless it's an emergency. I've no patience to sit here bouncing like a rubber ball answering phone calls in the afternoon when you workers go to the field and I'm left here all alone at my desk."

"What about Mrs. Ramsey, our unit clerk?" queries B-23. And the emergency worker. . ."

Mrs. Knox turns to face the offender abruptly. "I've no time to discuss the matter further, Mr. Gould," she says through clenched teeth while removing the receiver from the phone. "I've got to make a personal call."

Three days pass before a message from Mrs. Rivera breaks through the lines: Brodski is ill. It's an emergency. His mother says he needs you. My immediate thought: We shall see how much.

One day turns into two. Monday turns into Friday. A second week begins. Still I don't call or visit Brodski. Each morning the first thing I do when I arrive at the office, after signing Mrs. Knox's time sheet and delivering the paper, is empty my mail folder. After separating Mrs. Rivera's messages left the proceeding day from the other contents, I add them to an already impressive stack on my desk. I have let Mother's messages pile up. They give me great satisfaction. They assure me that my battle plan is working. Finally, after several heart-warming message-laden days more, something unexpected happens. Something I had hoped for but couldn't count on. Something only my great wealth of experience had led me to believe would occur.

The breakthrough comes in the form of a telephone call from Mrs. Thea Goldstein, Brodski's social worker at the Institute of Rehabilitation. She says that it will be necessary for Brodski to come into the hospital to have some special tests made on him. These tests cannot be given at home. Special equipment will have to be used. Will I be good enough to double-check with (and exert pressure on) Mrs. Rivera, she asks, so that no foul-up on the appointment date occurs. I answer: "I'll be only too happy to." There is more than satisfaction in my voice. There is gratitude.

On the day of Brodski's hospital appointment I visit his home. What a shame he is not there. Writing hurriedly I jot down in pencil a note for Mother on my Form W-26 and slip it under the door. In addition to my name and telephone number, the note indicates an urgent request for Mrs. Rivera to call me the next day. "We have something important to discuss," is the exact wording.

Promptly at 9:00 a. m. the following morning Mother calls. I tell her that if I can, I will visit her that afternoon. She replies anxiously, "Please, Mr. Haberman, please do." I answer, Why, of course, Mother dear, if there's any way possible for me to get out there, I will."

The appointment was made for 2:30 p.m.; I arrive at 4:00. Mother is haggard, pale, anxious. There is a suggestion of fear in her eyes. Brodski is glad to see me. If he could have, I could tell, he would have leaped for joy. Brusquely bypassing Mother, I enter his room. A present is in order. This time I have brought him a real prize. It is enough to make up for the long weeks of privation and pain he has had to endure through no fault of his own, but because of Mother. It is a projecting camera, screen and art slides of some of the world's most beautiful sites. The Pantheon, St. Paul's Cathedral, London, Grecian Ruins. Each slide has been handpicked by me. Specially chosen for its unique beauty. I want only the best for my darling on this occasion. The result is a veritable panapoly of the Seven Wonders of the World. Hadn't I promised as much earlier? With Mother waiting in her room, I spend hours with Brodski. I didn't even have to ask her to allow us to be alone. She consented of her own accord. Voluntarily. She understands these moments between the little one and me should be private. Hours go by. Not a word or sound passes between us. Not even the soft purring sound I have become accustomed to hearing when he is happy. Only the barely audible hum of the camera projector. The room is pitch dark. With each new slide I can sense Brodski becoming more and more enthralled. He devours them as a fat man does sweets. It is so easy to please him, I think. All you need to do is expose him to beauty. And the world has so much.

Each slide I have chosen is a superb work, the subject wonderfully captured by a photographic genius. Thus for a period covering more than four hours he shuttles from the ruins of ancient Greece to a modern glass-sheathed skyscraper; from the Cathedral de Notre Dame to the palatial villas of Uruguay. He sees these vistas as few others have seen them. Or at least have appreciated them. His gaze of religious wonder is only broken when he marvels at my dextrous fingers clicking the machine on and off or bringing each slide into perfect focus. It must seem something of a miracle to him. Don't forget, in his entire life he has never been to a movie. Or even watched TV. Mother won't permit him. No good for his eyes, I recollect her once telling me. Finally I deem it time to have my talk with Mother. I leave Brodski to observe Giotto's The Flight into Egypt and I enter her room.

My face projects a stern demeanor, even fierce, as I ask her to join me. "Here, sit beside me, darling, on this sofa. I have something important to discuss with you." And so, seated together on her sofa which in earlier days might have been a love seat, I sow the first seeds that will eventually decide the old lady's doom. Without explaining my behavior or the reasons for my withdrawal these last several weeks, I tell her *"THEY'VE"* decided to place a Home Attendant in her home to help care for Brodski. "They" feel this is an absolute necessity because of the medical reports "they" received only recently from the hospital.

Mother objects. The last thing she wants is a stranger coming into her home and caring for her child. Her reaction is precisely what I expected. I press my advantage at once. "The only alternative, Mother, would be for you to become Brodski's Home Attendant. I don't know if they will permit it, *but if you want me to,* I'll make the recommendation. Of course, it won't be easy. There's a real problem here. Relatives living with clients aren't generally allowed to serve as Home Attendant. The Department has strict

49

rules on that. But maybe if I can explain the extenuating circumstances and submit a special approval memo . . . well, maybe, just maybe. Of course, we won't tell anybody of your real relationship to Brodski. I mean that you're not even blood related. If they knew that, they just might decide to take him away from you altogether. Oh, don't worry. I won't tell. And I think I can pull this other thing off too. Anyway, It's certainly worth a try. Now, what do you say, Mother? Will you have a go at it?

The old lady looks at me askance. She hardly comprehends what I am saying. Probably the only words that do register are that "they" want to put a stranger in her home, and even worse, that "they" can take her child away from her.

"I don't want to get you into trouble, you understand, Mr. Haberman, but if you would be so kind to do what you say, I'd be very grateful."

The tone of her voice is meek, confused, pitiable. Her eyes moistened long ago. Hearing her speak and observing her now, naked as I do, on the love seat, an image flashes before me of a lovesick suitor begging for his beloved's hand. Nothing is more revolting. My voice gains strength as I respond.

"Why, of course, Mother darling. No trouble at all. I only hope I can gain approval for you. I'm convinced you'd be an excellent Home Attendant. And you know something—there's a good deal of extra money in it for you. Home Attendant's make $3.35 an hour, and you'll be working full time. Twenty-four hours per day. Though you'll only get paid for twelve. Can't help that. That's the policy. But then, you'll be getting meal allowance and carfare."

By her reaction it is apparent that Mother isn't interested in the money. But is that really true? Though she shook her head doggedly, indicating fierce dissapproval, I thought I detected just a hint of disappointment when she heard me say that Home Attendant's don't get paid for more than a twelve-hour work day even if they work twenty-four hours. Or am I imagining things?

Taking her by the arm I lead her to my next point.

"Here, now Mother, before I go, let me teach you how to work this photo machine so you can show Brodski the same beautiful pictures when I'm gone. After all, I can't be here all the time and you know how the little one just loves to look at them."

Together we enter his room. Brodski is still gazing devoutly at the slide of The Flight into Egypt, as he was when I left him at least thirty minutes earlier. His expression is a fusion of ecstasy, wonder and awe. He seems hypnotized. Mother turns soft looking down at him. She smiles. All will be well are the words etched across her face. I demonstrate to her how to work the machine. After supper that evening she promise me (and him) that she will again show Brodski my slides.

Before leaving, I collect the slides I have shown to Brodski and replace them with a different set. These are not so pretty. Some are the same slides I have already exhibited with a defect in them—perhaps they are slightly darkened due to a lack of light when shot or a different exposure, or less distinct because the camera had moved when shooting. Also I have included a few slides haphazardly that are worth no more attention than an everyday Brownie snapshot.

I have to call upon all my strength to go, realizing only too well what I am going to miss later than evening. The exquisite expressions on Brodski's face (and Mother's in response to his) when he views these horrors; the squeals and cat cries that will dominate the room when Mother in utter futility makes every effort to bring these slides into sharper focus.

Poor thing: Only I can bring joy to Brodski's household. Only I can bear Brodski beauty. Mother, it seems, can cause only pain. What will Brodski be thinking? For that matter, what will Mother? She doesn't have any idea I exchanged the slides. And even if her son knew, which he doesn't, he couldn't tell her.

The amazing thing is not how much we expect when we're young—when we're starting out—but how little we end up with as adults. And yet it's enough. We adjust. We make the best of it. We live our lives! . . . Do we?

*Xerox copy placed in manuscript; original word union made by Haberman:

ni-hil-ism (ni'e lis'em, ne'-), n. 1. total rejection of established laws and institutions. 2. Philos, a. an extreme form of skepticism: the denial of all real existence or the possibility of an objective basis for truth. b. nothingness or nonexistence. c. See ethical nihilism. 3. (sometimes cap.) the principles of a Russian revolutionary group, active in the latter half of the 19th century, holding that existing social and political institutions must be destroyed in order to clear the way for a new state of society and employing extreme measures, including terrorism, and assassination. 4. anarchy, terrorism, or other revolutionary activity. 5. annihilation of the self, or the individual consciousness, esp. as an aspect of mystical experience. 6. total and absolute destructiveness, esp. toward the world at large and including oneself: the power-mad nihilism that so strongly marked Hitler's last years. (Nihil + -ism) -ni'hil-ist, n., adj. -ni'hil-is'tic, adj.

Aes-thete (es'thet or, esp. Brit., es-) n. 1. one who has or professes to have a high degree of sensitivity toward the beauties of art or nature. 2. one who affects great love of art, music, poetry, etc, and indifference to practical matters. Also, esthete. Gk aisthetes, one who perceives, equiv. to aisthe- (var. s. of aisthanesthai to perceive) + tes n. suffix denoting agent) -Syn. 1. connoisseur. 2. dillettante.

N-I-H-I-L-E-S-T-H-E-T-E

52

At the office the next day Mrs. Knox is vehemently against allowing Brodski's mother to be made Home Attendant. "Clearly the Department's policy regarding relatives being made Home Attendants couldn't be more *clear.* Especially those relatives already living with the clients and performing the functions free."

"But Mrs. Rivera's not really a relative, Mrs. Knox. Just a sort of volunteer foster mother. And we both know it's an unusual case. A special situation."

My "buts" continue well into the morning. Finally, after what must seem like psychopathic persistence on my part, she relents.

"If you want to take the time to write"—she grits her teeth—"an Exception to Policy Memo, Mr. Haberman, requesting special approval for this client, I won't stand in your way. But remember one thing, Mr. Haberman. You'll have to type the memo yourself. I'm not going to ask Tonita to type it. I wouldn't dare think of wasting our office typist's time on something like this."

"Thank you, Mrs. Knox." (Thank you very much).

This much going to task for a client is nonexistent in the Department. Not only does it require a great deal of extra work in the actual drafting of the memo, gathering of facts and details, careful choice of words, and adherence to precise instructions regarding memo form and structure (Procedure 2-587), but Exception to Policy Memos are rarely, if ever, approved by case consultation anyway. And why should they be? Every time the Department puts its stamp of approval on anything it costs the city money. So departmental policy is to unequivocally say *no* to everything. (The unwritten but all-encompassing law of Civil

53

Service Land). But I can manage it, I think to myself. All I need is a strong letter from Dr. Umano at the Institute of Rehab—Thea Goldstein can manage that. And certainly soliciting the support of the Director won't hurt either. He just L-O-V-E-S the bonsai tree I got him. I am a Field General, Foot Soldier, and Specialist in Intelligence . . . but my true place in the army is in executing "maneuvers."

Three weeks later, after a barrage of phone calls from case consultation requesting followup memos and information, after overcoming bureaucratic red tape ad infinitum, Special Approval is granted for Maria Rivera to become Home Attendant.

I don't ask Mother's permission to take Brodski outdoors yet. Instead I wait for her to receive her first Home Attendant check. This is part of my strategy. Perhaps the most important part of my battleplan.

One hour after she cashed the check (I followed her to the bank; our IBM printout sheet on check rolls told me when the check would be delivered) I visited her at home. She was busy preparing the evening meal. What is this: a new set of dishes, Mother? And a matching pair of aprons for you and your son? My, my, Mother, if you're not a big spender, you're certainly a fast one. Oh, well, as they say, "easy come, easy go."

Almost before I enter her apartment, she senses something is wrong. I appear frantic as the words pour from my mouth.

"Mother, Mother, we made a terrible mistake," I lie. "I just learned that "they" can take your son away from you if you do something illegal such as become Home Attendant. I had no idea the rules and regulations were that punitive, but they are. You must not for a moment serve in this household as a Home Attendant. Nor cash one single Home Attendant check. If you do, I don't know what they'll do to you. Yes, I do! *THEY'LL TAKE YOUR CHILD AWAY FROM YOU!*"

Mother peers at me incredulously. Some sort of pre-reflective survival mechanism pushes ordered sentences from her mouth even though her face is a miasma of confusion.

"But you said it would be all right, Mr. Haberman. You said you would take care of everything. Now what should I do?"

"But I will, Mother, and I have. All you have to do is

resign your post as Home Attendant. I'll tell them I spoke to you and you reconsidered. Realizing your error, you decided you didn't want to take one dollar from the Department. And you haven't."

"Haven't what, Mr. Haberman?"

"Haven't stolen one dollar, Mother. After all, you haven't yet cashed a single check, have you?"

Her face turns ashen. Her jaw slackens. She seems about to faint. I seize the opportunity to let my eyes wander about the apartment.

"Mother! What's this? I don't remember ever seeing these dishes before. And these aprons, Mother! Where and when did you get them?"

She does faint. Ka-plomp. In a large, heavy wooden kitchen chair. Her voice, too, goes limp.

"Just an hour or so ago, Mr. Haberman. In the . . . in the G & S General Store on Lexington Avenue and 116th Street. I . . . I cashed the check I received this morning and then I went to the store and I purchased . . ."

"YOU WHAT!?!"

My words grip her like a vice. She opens her mouth to say something but she can't. She is like a mute groping for sound. Only the effort is there.

The look on my face tells her what she already knows. That she has done the worst.

"Oh, Mother," I yell, "how can I save you now? You cashed the check. You committed a crime. We can't even return it. And you . . . you even spent the money. *They'll definitely take your child!!!*"

I tear the apron from her middle and crumple it in my hands. Tears stream from her eyes. A soul-searing cry vocally the equivalent of Munch's anguished vision issues from her lips. She collapses in my arms.

It took me almost two hours to apease her. I had to call upon my cumulative years of experience and not inconsiderable powers of persuasion to do so. My biggest fear was that I wouldn't be able to dissuade her from using her own money to pay the Department back. I had to convince her that the Department would look upon that act only as a mere gesture, and never agree to accept her money as restitution. A crumbled, dog-eared newspaper clipping I just happen to have had with me illustrating a situation in which a recipient attempted to make up stolen funds with her own meager savings was all the proof I needed. "No, Mother," I said with just the right tone of emphasis, "the Department is neither lenient nor understanding in these situations. And understandably so. They've been burnt too many times in the past by real criminals. Why, it's been documented that just last year millions of dollars were stolen by clients alone."

From that point on it was easy. As Mother sat in a fetal position in her wooden chair, convulsed with sobs, I explained over and over how I wouldn't tell anybody what she had done. How fortunate she was I was her caseworker. How if we stuck together on this, we could beat the Department, the cruel system. "No, Mother. Nobody's going to take your son away from you. Not as long as I'm your caseworker, they won't. You have my solemn word on that. *I promise!*"

That evening I stayed with Brodski for the first time till well into the night. Mother went to the movies with a friend. Why not? She has the money now and *I insisted!*

Bundled in a warm, brown woolen army blanket and strapped to his wheelchair, the little fellow has been outside each afternoon for the past several weeks. As I expected, the more he gets to see of the world, the more of himself he begins to discover. And the closer I get to discovering him. Brodski never seems to tire of this interchange. Nor do I. There are but two unvarying rules to our daily excursions. One is: He sees only the beautiful. If I see a doddering old lady, humped over in a crab crawl on the other side of the street, or a man with an enlarged goiter, or even a dog raising its hind leg or squatting on its haunches, or worse, its master shoveling up its leftovers, I whisk Brodski away as if he were a Jew in Germany, the year '39, and the Gestapo coming. For Brodski, the world must seem like Marco Polo's Venetia, and I like Marco Polo. On each trip I bestow on him untold riches to behold. Second rule: He must know I am solely responsible for his daily joys. Mother is not and never has been. Each turn of his wheelchair reminds him of this rule. By the way I push it, at which angle I hold it, move it forward or don't move it forward, do an about-face, come to an abrupt halt, Brodski comes to realize that if he is on wheels, I am the driver. The starter, steering wheel and brakes are mine to control.

With such power at my disposal it sometimes takes great restraint to stop myself from denying Brodski. Like when we were at the museum last week. He had just spent two hours meticulously scrutinizing an exhibition of thirteenth century Columbian handiwork, and then, when I ushered him upstairs to see Picasso's Guernica, I could swear the little fellow had an orgasm. One slight twist or turn to the right or to the left and his world would have grown dark. Literally disappeared. But I don't succumb to temptation. I have few virtues but one of them is self-discipline. Without that, nothing.

That doesn't mean I'm not subject to human error. Accidents will happen. For example, after allowing Brodski so many minutes to see Guernica, was it my fault I tripped and sustained an ankle sprain? That we had to leave prematurely? Surely, he couldn't blame me for that. Nor could he hold a grudge. Not when early the next morning—it was Saturday and I had no work—I returned with him to the museum to view his precious painting. It was the first time I ever spent the weekend (or part of it) with Brodski. He learned several very important lessons that day. Once again, he learned who is master, who controls his fate. And he also learned of my benevolence and the fact that he can count on my word. For I had assured him the previous night that we would return.

58

Have you ever noticed how an absolute stranger standing in an elevator will find it impossible to prevent himself from laying hands on a beautiful child? The need to caress the child's cheek is overwhelming. It seems the most natural thing in the world. Such is the power of beauty. This is the way Brodski sees the world. Everywhere we go he sees beautiful children. If only he had hands to caress them.

Not for the first time (that was something special, just for Brodski and myself) but the second, or perhaps the third time out, I allowed Mother to join us. I knew she was curious about our little trips and felt left out, and who was I to say no? On that occasion Brodski was not so fortunate. His aesthetic expectations did not fare so well. No museum, city landmark, or Manhattan skyline did he see that day. Poor fellow. Who could foretell Mother's idea of "fun" would be to take him for a walk on Fifth Avenue? In Harlem! From 118th Street all the way up to . . . Brodski was positively ruined by the time he returned home that evening. He lay crumpled in his crib, shattered and mute. I never thought he'd recover or go out again. The filth, the stench, the poverty of Harlem, Mother did not miss a thing. The cries of the cat cascaded that afternoon in Harlem with as much force as a tidal wave. Every resident for blocks around stuck his beady-eyed black head out the window. They knew we were there. How could they not know? In addition to the startling range of Brodski's vocal cords, his tears in sheer volume must have equaled a record N.Y.C. downpour.

The trip didn't do Mother much good either. Since that time she hasn't asked to join us again. Not that Brodski misses her. Now, whenever I come to take him out, he gives her such a peculiar look it could only mean one thing: Stay home! And I quote him correctly. You can bet the little tyrant never says please. I am, of course, not so impolite. Knowing the way Mother feels, I would never suggest a repeat performance, though. Besides being unnecessary, it would be in bad taste to dupe her again so soon.

Mother's itinery of Harlem would have had a similar effect on anybody, not only one as sensitive as Brodski. I, for instance, when making my field visits always walk with my nose buried in a newspaper or book so I won't have to witness some junkie reeling in his stupor, or a wino slobbering at the mouth, or some other irredeemable social unfortunate making ready to mug me or put a shiv in my gut. If he does, he does! There's little I or anybody else can do about it. Thats the way it is. Today! So far, I count my blessings. Ever since I've worked for the Department, I've only been accosted in the field three times. (Four if you want to include an argument that led to fisticuffs which I really was more responsible for than not). In any event, I know of no better way to show my contempt for the residents of Harlem than not to notice them. One thing blacks have in common with all disenfranchised groups is that they have to be recognized. Have a name. Ask any cop on the beat what happens if he doesn't refer to them by name. The appellation "Hey you!" is enough to start a race riot. I guess they've been invisible too long. My own problems of anonymity is of an entirely different origin.

Seeing the way Brodski responds to the world, I am reminded of my father when he went to Paris after many years of saving and prodding by my mother. I shall never forget his grandiloquent summation when he returned.

"So what do you think, Abe?" asked Uncle Tom. How did you like Paris?"

"Paris! Who needs Paris," was his reply. "I had to travel two thousand miles in discomfort and spend all that money to see a lousy river. Tell me, Tom, what's the difference between the Seine and the Hudson? . . . I'll tell you. There is none!"

Only Brodski is not my father. Rather he is like a newborn infant. He sees everything as if for the first time. He marvels at positively everything. There is nowhere I can

60

take him that is better than another. That is not to say that he does not discriminate. He still continues to dismiss the ordinary and the commonplace with disdain. I still have to shield him from unpleasant sights. It is just that with his new found exposure to the outside world he has grown to the point where he can find something of value everywhere. Each place and sight has its own special worth to him. Its own miracle. But it is all so ill-defined. Just how ill-defined came as a surprise even to me.

I was rolling Brodski up the ramp to the museum the other day for the umpteenth time when he let out a soft whimper. I hardly noticed at first and continued to climb, when to my surprise I heard him again. Looking down at him, I realized that his utterance was really a cry of protest. The little fellow was objecting to going into the museum. Something else had caught his eye. What? Impelled by a sense of urgency, I turned around. Maybe I could learn something from this. It was midafternoon and the area was only sparsely populated with what seemed to me a few inconsequential pedestrians walking the streets. I continued to gaze around, half hoping, half knowing, that this incident might be the first real turn of events since I had begun taking him outdoors more than a month ago. So far nothing out of the ordinary had happened. So far I had only learned from him pretty much what I already knew. With this in mind I searched the streets eagerly but nothing appeared. Nothing showed itself. So what was it that drew his attention? Finally it dawned upon me. Sitting on the other side of the street in front of an old brownstone, slightly obstructed by a large tree, was an ancient lady in a wheel chair with her Home Attendant standing erect by her side. The ancient lady wore a wide-brimmed straw hat and was wrapped in a multicolored patchwork quilt, and the Home Attendant was shading her from the sun by holding a parasol over her. The ancient lady had bony, stooped shoulders, a face so old it was young, ghostly white, heavily veined papyrus hands, and legs, exposed from the knees down, made of the same or similar material: lacking musculature and tone, seemingly held together by varicose veins and layers of stretched rubbery skin. Not a pretty sight. So what could have captured Brodski's attention? At first I thought it was simply the fact that he identified with her. That she was a wheelchair victim like himself with a woman (Mother) caring for her.

But it wasn't that. Only the day before I had to rush him away from another person in a wheelchair, also old, also accompanied by a female Home Attendant, because he reacted so badly upon seeing her.

My second guess seemed closer to the mark. Perhaps he found the old lady's patchwork quilt especially beautiful, and it was. More like a tapestry. Even I thought it a waste to use as a mere blanket. But it wasn't that either. With the midday sun strongly beating down on the old woman, the Home Attendant had occasion to remove the quilt from her lap; but Brodski continued to stare! Now I was really baffled. If it wasn't that, what was it? I must have asked myself that question a hundred times in those few minutes, each time becoming more puzzled and confused, each time feeling that the answer to my question was vitally important if I was to gain a more complete understanding of Brodski.

At last I realized what it was. Brodski was seeing a picture. A beautiful quintessentially self-contained frame of: Servant Holding a Parasol Over Her Mistress. The painting (if painted) could have been from another century. It was worthy of Renoir or any of the great French Impressionists. Brodski, the little darling, had seen a picture in real life. Not one already made by an artist, but one that might have inspired the artist in the first place. His wonderfully sensitive eye had caught something neither mine nor anybody else's—other than an artist's—would have seen.

From that point on I was no good either to Brodski or myself. Through our entire tour of the museum only one thought raced through my mind. I couldn't wait to return home to decipher the meaning of what had just been revealed to me, to study how I could take advantage of it. Exploit it. Render it useful. I paid Brodski little or no attention the rest of the day. I did not anticipate his whimpers of protestation. Only after some delay did I respond to his directives to make a left or right turn, to stand still or

62

go forward. Brodski looked at me strangely more than once.

When Mother called me late that evening and alluded to his bad mood I thought I was the cause for his distemper.

It was still some time before I found out how wrong I was.

After much deliberation I have decided on a new course of action. No longer will I expose Brodski to beautiful sites alone. Museums, skylines, landmarks, art exhibitions, will no longer be our exclusive domain. From here on I will not take Brodski anywhere. He will take me. I will walk along the streets of New York like a hunter trailing his hound dog and he will tell me where to stop, what to see, what is of consequence and what is not. This is the best way, I have decided, if I am ever to truly discover who Brodski is. As always: I am on the hunt for Brodski.

Nothing he sees can he give a name. He has never learned words to describe anything. Objects are not representations or even symbols assigned to linguistic conventions to him. They are only pure images. Oh, if only he could tell me what he sees.

But he will.

It is my job to make him.

Strange: Now that I have given him leeway in leading me around I have at the same time tightened my hold on the reins. Maybe it isn't so strange. I don't want Brodski to miss a thing. And I don't want to miss Brodski.

Is not all art made of the same two opposing tensions? Absolute freedom and classical restraint?

If I am an artist . . . my art is Brodski.

So I have taken Brodski out of his wheelchair and carry him now in a papoose. I got the idea from observing a young mother carrying her child in just this way. With

Brodski snugly fitted in this satchel, a kind of marsupial pouch, it's easier for me to follow his movements. Or for him to control mine. He's truly now an extension of me, as I am a part of him. If he as much as quivers, my entire system quakes. We are what I always hoped we would be: One.

If I cannot discover the mystery of who he is now, I never will. Come darling, show me who you are. Only then can the real game begin.

Guess where he takes me. Of all the places in the city we always end up at the same site. The Maine Monument! Once there, all cries, purrs, mewing sounds, even scarcely perceptible squirmings of his body cease. He goes into a trance. The only thing that exists for him then is the artist who does her sketches in chalk. By now she is quite accomplished. Her chalk arabesques of Christ and other holy figures reflect a certain felicity of style along with a rigid adherence to technique. The Chalk Artist always has a large crowd surrounding her and her rumpled brown paper bag is always filled to the edge with money. But Brodski pays little heed to the crowd or to the money. He is held spellbound by the artist at her work. He can lose himself for hours at a time watching her, and does (he refuses to go home with me until she is done) oblivious of all else: time, people, children gamboling about, the elements, have no effect on him. I'm convinced I have never seen him happier than at those moments.

Why, then, when we return home does his mood change so drastically? I am almost afraid to leave him alone with Mother and more often than not do not. It starts when we leave the artist, and by the time we're home, he's bleak, wan, dissolute, uncontrollably temperamental. There is no talking to him. Nothing I say or do affects him.

Mother feels equally helpless at theses times and is actually grateful when I stay on. Still, she takes these opportunities to wag her finger at me. "I knew no good would come of your taking him outside, Mr. Haberman," she moans. I can only respond by telling her the truth. "On the contrary, Mother dear, this afternoon he was fine. Up until the moment we left for home he was perfectly happy. In fact, to be perfectly honest, I have never seen him so happy. It's quite evident his dark moods must have something to do with his returning home. Both of us should admit that much."

But I know this is not the whole truth, either. There is a clue here, a symptom; but what is it? Something profound is disturbing him. The artist? The trip back home? Figures of Christ? What is it?

I must find out.

One evening I send Mother off to play bingo with her friend at a church function. She goes out quite frequently now. Maybe two or three times a week. Brodski and I spend these nights together until she returns. This evening I have decided to try something. My aim is to determine whether it is the artist's pictures or the creative process itself that fascinates Brodski. For that reason I have purchased one of those Paint-Yourself-by-the-Numbers kits. As the instructions are easy to follow, and the colors furnished quite eyecatching, I am flattered by the result. My drawing (I won't say creation) of a pastoral landscape is really quite good. Brodski is not as impressed as I. His mood is just as sullen now when I have finished as it was earlier when I began. There is even a hint of mocking disdain on his little bird's face.

Well, then, at least I have learned this much: his mood changes have something to do with the artistic process, the mystery of creation. How else could you explain his utter contempt for my drawing, which in all fairness is at least as pleasing to the eye as some of the Chalk Artist's lesser efforts, except that the little devil knew I was cheating? I am satisifed. I have trod another step on my Road to Damascus.

65

That night I fall asleep muttering the words: "But what does it mean?"

Doesn't it always happen this way? Purely by accident, when least expected. Once a week someone in the unit is designated "E" worker and cannot leave the office under any circumstances *all day*. Mrs. Knox never deviates from her schedule. You could have a real "E"-mergency in your home. Your father, mother, brother, sister, wife, child, could be sick, mugged, raped, dying, dead, but on "E" day you don't leave the office. Mrs. Knox won't allow you to. As luck would have it, today was my day to be "Emergency Worker." Of course, if it didn't happen this way, it would have happened another. Brodski already had planted the seeds. They were germinating inside me just waiting to sprout. It was just a matter of when the plant would grow, the flowers bloom.

And after lunch time today they did!

As always, it started with Mother. It seems the more time I spend with Broadki, the more greedy for money she becomes for doing less work. Lately, in addition to doing my usual housekeeping chores, cleaning the apartment, adjusting and focusing the lights on his paintings, centering them, dusting and even doing the ironing, laundry and some cooking, I've also assumed a good portion of her Home Attendant duties. And she knows it. In the evenings, even when she is there, it's I who bathes the little fellow and then puts him to bed. Of course I use these hours to good advantage. For instance, I have learned that when in the bath, he doesn't respond any more to a Ruben's nude than he does to a *Penthouse* centerfold; the erotic imagination is really quite lacking in him. But the way he responds to touch is something else. When I fondle his privates and watch his member grow to a size it's impossible beforehand to imagine; or the way he screws up his face and shuts his eyes and squeals for joy with his whole body seeming to knot up in a ball of concentrated delight, it never fails to get me laughing nearly as loudly as he wails. Also the warm water and suds, (the soapier the better), the touch of my hands on his body—these are the things he loves. If he lacks erotic imagination, there's no doubt he's tactile. Perhaps he just doesn't know how to associate pictures with actual sex. After all, he hasn't had any experience. My touch (and Mother's) are the only sexual pleasures he knows. I must admit when I stroke him, I, too, realize some pleasure. Though it would be remiss to call it sexual. I get the same feeling, though not as intense, when holding a butterfly by the wing before letting it go, or crushing it between my fingers, depending upon my whim.

When Mother came into my office this afternoon complaining of not having received her Home Attendant check, I was surprised because she brought Brodski with her. She could have taken him first to a friend, but the moment her mailman told her "No check," she couldn't wait to get to the center. It just goes to show how far greed has taken her; and dissatisfaction. Only two short months ago she was on her knees begging me not to take him outside. And now this. For a few paltry dollars, she exposes him to the riffraff of a welfare center. I didn't remonstrate or lecture her, though. That's not my way. There's nothing to be gained by that. Instead I took hold of a handle on Brodski's wheelchair with one hand, and Mother's arm with my other, and steered them both away from the reception area to my desk, all the while assuring her that everything would be all right. At my desk I introduced her to Mrs. Knox. It was the first time my Supervisor (and the rest of my unit, who just sat qawking. Even when it's not their "E" day they don't take advantage of fieldtime) met Mrs. Rivera and Brodski, and even she was a bit ruffled. Some primordial human spark ignited eons back now flickered in her.

Addressing Mrs. Knox, but making certain to speak loudly enough for all concerned to hear, I say, "Look at this, Mrs. Knox. Isn't this typical of the Department.

Here's a woman who works harder than anybody else and the Department doesn't even pay her."

Mrs. Knox rises from her desk, walks over to mine and bids me go fetch the replacement-of-lost-check forms while she picks up where I left off in comforting my client. As I take my leave I can hear her say, "Don't you worry now, Mrs. Rivera. All we need is for you to sign the lost-check forms and have our notary witness your signature. Once you do that, Mr. Haberman will be able to replace your check in no time."

After returning to my desk with the proper forms, I leave Brodski and escort Mrs. Rivera to another floor to seek out a notary. On the elevator I continue to put her at ease, spelling out what I know she needs to hear. "No, Mother," I say, "I don't blame you one iota for thinking the way you do. For wanting money. The finer things in life. In fact, I admire you for it. A parent has got to be crazy to make her children her entire life in today's world. There's no reward in that. Not with kids the way they are today. When they grow up, they leave you. They don't even look back. Why, just look at your own. He's no exception. And to think, all the love and care you frittered away on that ingrate. All the years of sacrifice you spent on him. I'm telling you, Mother, the best thing you can do for yourself is to enjoy the few years you have left. Don't worry about Brodski. He can take care of himself. Or better yet, he's got a softie like me to do it for him. And to think, only a few short months ago he didn't even know I existed."

After another hour Brodski and Mother (check safely deposited in her purse) were ready to leave the office, when those aforementioned wholly unexpected things began to happen.

To begin with, Mrs. Knox transcended her rigid strictures by going against departmental policy and recommending that we issue carfare allowance to Mrs. Rivera and Brodski. "But Mrs. Knox," I exclaimed in utter disbelief, "you know my clients live within walking distance of the center. We're forbidden to give them any money for transportation."

"Show a little understanding, Mr. Haberman," Mrs.

Knox responded in an indignant tone. "It's already late. In a short while it will be dark out. Besides, you can't really expect a senior citizen like Mrs. Rivera to walk your client home in a wheelchair." She paused. Second thoughts? Hedging the bet? "I'll tell you what, Mr.Haberman. Go speak to your Office Liason. Tell Mr. Becker that if it's all right with him, it's all right with me."

Surprised? I was too shocked to be surprised. Besides who was I, a lowly caseworker, to argue with my Supervisor?

Hans Becker is a European Jew out of a concentration camp with the blue numbers on his arm to prove it. From Austrian Aristocracy to Auschwitz. A complete reversal of lifestyles. After he saw the Old World die, he dedicated every nerve ending of feeling he had left to helping to build the new. Residents of Harlem stand to profit from this historical synaptical connection.

He once held the lofty position of Director, but has long since been demoted to low man on the totem pole: Office Laison. His greatest crime was that he said "yes" to everything. Each time a member of his staff asked, "Can I give Mrs. Smith a grant for household replacements?" Yes. "Moving expenses?" Yes. "Winter clothing?" Yes. "Summer camp?" Yes. "Three months' rent in advance, security deposit and brokers fee?" Yes.

The downtown financial analysts felt shivers run up and down their collective spines. After auditing Hans' welfare center's monthly grant total for eight months straight and comparing it to all other centers throughout the city, one even went so far as to send a memo to the Mayor's office claiming that Hans was the single biggest reason why the city of New York was chronically in the red. That was Hans' downfall. Now the only thing they let him say yes to is requests for transportation allowance. He can approve no more than a token or two.

However, that's not the way Hans perceives his position. He figures his change-of-work life was a blessing in disguise. With such a reduction in his work responsibility, he

69

can now devote himself exclusively to his extracurricular ("shady," to quote recent memos from downtown) activities. In short, he can help "the people" full time. Despite all his love and care for his black brothers and sisters, though, our Office Liaison has massive attacks of fear. Hans Becker never leaves the office at 5 p.m. alone. He's terrified to do so. He'll stay three hours overtime without pay waiting for the night watchman to walk him to the subway station, or even better, a fellow worker to drive him home. The blue marks are printed in more ways than one.

After interrupting our Office Liaison from what seemed like one of his shadier projects (he was conversing with a large man with a flaming red beard and black beret—judging from his words, an artist—about joining him in his battle to create an art exhibition here in Harlem) and telling him (actually I demonstrated it; Brodski and Mother accompanied me into his office) of my request for transportation, he grabbed me jubilantly in a bear hug and kissed my forehead. "You surprise me, Robert. I always knew you were a good caseworker, but this . . . we should all give such love to our clients. I was just telling Leo here, we need more men like him (and you) in Harlem. Not like those robots downtown. They've no love in them. They're not human beings. They won't even let me use my regular office hours to set up an art show with Leo. Of course"—he smiles, returning to his desk—"I don't have to listen to them."

In such a way I received carfare allowance for Mother and Brodski. Unplanned? Wholly unexpected? To be sure. But now for the real kicker. The *coup de grace*. Not wanting to detain my Office Liason and his artist friend any longer, (not only are we interrupting Becker's meeting but it seems from a few words muttered by the artist that he's looking forward to a belated lunch), I turn towards the door. Mrs. Rivera has already stashed the two tokens in her change purse and there is no further reason to stay. Our business is over. But Brodski won't leave. Once again, something has caught his eye. He is staring fixedly at the Office Liaison's desk. What is it this time? The Office

Liaison's desk is no different from any other; just an ordinary gray metallic office desk, the kind you see in every office. Notes, paper, case records piled on top. Two bins, one for incoming material, the other for out going. Nothing out of the ordinary. So what has captured his attention this time? There is no artist at work here, no creative process being unfolded, nothing beautiful to see. So what now?

More than ever I am baffled, and embarrassed too. I'm holding Becker and his friend up and I feel a slow burn beginning to smolder on my neck. Putting my full weight against Brodski's wheelchair, I commence to forcefully push him out the door. But he lets out such a shrill cry that the entire fifth floor reverberates with sound. And even though we are halfway out the door, by some peculair arrangement of neck vertebrae that enables him to turn his head at a 270-degree angle, he turns around and continues to gawk in the direction of the Office Liaison's desk. I am peering at him dumbfounded when the Office Liaison rises from his desk chair, strides over to Brodski, squats down, and attempts to line up his sightline with whatever seems to be holding his attention. Then, bouncing up jauntily, and half muttering to himself, Becker announces, "The poor boy must be hungry." He hastily retreats to his desk, and after hesitating for a fraction, removes a banana lying between an apple and a plum, and begins peeling away its skin. He then offers it to Brodski holding it up temptingly just a few inches in front of his face.

Alas, Brodski's plaintive wailing only grows worse. He stretches and twists his neck to what appears to be several inches beyond its limit in an obvious effort not to lose eye contact with what continues to hold his gaze. Pivoting on his heels to face his artist friend, the Office Liaison says, "So what do you think, Leo? You've got the artistic eye. There's something about my desk upsetting him. What is it?"

Artist not saint, Leo Byron, laughs in malicious glee. "I don't know about the retard, Hans, but I'll tell you what all his shrieking and crying has drawn my eye to. That damn chicken leg I brought over wrapped in aluminum foil heating up on the radiator. It's a perfect still life. Oh, sure, for a few seconds I thought it was the apple, plum and banana lying on your desk. To tell you the truth, I was even thinking of doing a repeat of a Cézanne still life with them. But no more. That damn chicken leg's not only given me an original subject, but opened me up to a whole new way of looking at things. A new form. I've even got a name for it. 'Civil Service Lunch.' But seeing it's only one thing. Damn, I've got to paint it! My God, if I can put this on canvas," he continues while walking over to the radiator and taking the chicken leg gingerly in his huge hands, "I could not only surpass anything ever done by Cezanne, but by anyone else, right on up to Picasso. But I guess only an artist sees things this way. I'll be damned if I know what got into that freak of yours."

But I do!!!

From the moment I hear his words, "But seeing it's only one thing. Damn, I've got to paint it," they ring in my ears like a litany. And when he lifts the chicken leg from the radiator and Brodski quiets down, my head begins to reel from the shock of discovery. I can't wait for the day to end, to visit Brodski at home, to spend time with Brodski alone and luxuriate in my joy. Now it is the Office Liaison who is detaining me. I hear him calling my name as if from a distance. "Oh, Robert," he says, "today's your "E" day, isn't it? Will you be kind enough to walk me to the subway after work?"

"I'm sorry, Mr. Becker," I answer, my head still spinning, but I was planning to visit Brodski later."

"But that would be after five o'clock, Robert. What are you going to do, work overtime?"

"Not actually paid overtime, Mr. Becker. But as you can see, Brodski requires all the attention I can give him."

"Shall I wait for you to return to the office then, Robert?" he persues me. His voice betrays him. It's got an anxious lilt to it. "Will your visit be long?"

I do an about-face and confront the Office Liason squarely in the eyes. "The answer to your first question is no, Becker. And to your second, yes."

SO BRODSKI'S AN ARTIST! He must have told me in a thousand ways already, only I've been too stupid or too blind to see it. What else could he be? What else could all his mood changes and inner transports have meant? And his artist's eye. He sees the world only in images. My God, what pain and frustration he must have endured each time he saw a thing of beauty and wasn't able to express his own. But I shall remedy that, little one. All you need are the tools to create. And I will give them to you. Arms, and more importantly, hands, shall be yours.

Now where shall I find them?

How could I have been so blind?

It is Regina Dailey, our Medical Social Worker, who came to the rescue. I had wasted the better part of a week in the medical libraries and with a half dozen physical therapists and rehabilitation specialists who either were remiss in keeping appointments or begrudged me their time. Besides, they know less than I do, and the medical libraries are for students, scholars and theoreticians, not men of practical interests like myself. But Regina Dailey leads me right to the source. Before the words are half out of my mouth she removes from the bottom drawer of her desk the *Abbey Medical Rehabilitation Equipment Catalog,* and lays it before me. Leafing through the pages, I feel a thrill shoot through me from sole to soul. It is just what I need. "Where can I get it?" I ask her excitedly. "No need," she says. "Take mine. You can borrow mine for as long as you need it. You're the first caseworker who's shown a genuine interest in his client in my three and a half years here. If you can help one client, I'd gladly handprint a dozen more."

I don't need more. One is enough. For me this equipment catalog is a more priceless treasure than all of Shakespeare's sonnets, science's monographs, and the world's great literature combined. That evening I study the book anxiously. There is more here than I ever thought I'd need to know. All kinds of aids besides arms and hands to help Brodski realize his fate. Before going to sleep I think myself fortunate to live in an age where the human body and virtually all its parts can be so easily replaced. Only the soul cannot be. And that is my province. Not sciences'. I don't require help there.

There are advantages to everything. Even working for the Department. The most obvious is field time. A five-minute telephone contact with a client can furnish me with sufficient information to justify an hour's field visit. Often, all I need to know is that the client is alive (even I cannot visit a deceased client and get away with it . . . Mrs. Knox keeps statistics on expiration dates too). If alive, the client rates a visit, and I record one on my W712. Allowing time for travel, not-at-home visits (that's when no one's at home; at least I say no one was) and innovative collaterals (interviews with a nonexistent super, nameless neighbor, a phantom hospital social worker, a man on the door step), I can account for a full afternoon's work with maybe thirty minutes' worth of phone calls. In thirty-four years, I'd say I never made more than ten to twenty per cent of the field visits I've been credited for. My full forty-hour work week cost me less than twenty.

Of course, not all caseworkers are as bold as me. Richard Gould, for example, would never do anything "so dishonest" as to fabricate a field contact. "I could get caught! Anyway, I like visiting my clients." He spends half the day asking me for advice on how to record the visits he does make. "If I leave at 12 'clock, Haberman, how many visits do I have to make?" or one 'clock? Or two? three? four? Another of his daily queries concerns the advantages of eating lunch before or after he leaves for the field. No matter how many times I tell him he can eat first and still

74

record it on his time card when he does leave for the field as L & F (Lunch and Field) and that no one will know the difference, he never does. His greatest dilemma comes on payday. "I'm going to the field before I get my check," he says. "I don't like walking around with it."

"So why go to the field?" I reply. "Go home. Or better yet, treat yourself. It's payday. Go to the movies."

He doesn't even answer.

Every morning he gets on the phone with a client and says "Good morning, Mrs. Riddick. I'm just calling to make sure you'll be home this afternoon. I'd like to visit you some time after lunch, say around . . ." the words grate on my mind like chalk on slate. But I don't let it bother me. The world is full of Richard Goulds. I'm not like them and never would be. The only tragedy of my life is that I have so few ways to exhibit my talents other than robbing the Department of field time. But I make up for it in other ways. At least I try.

Another advantage of working for the Department is . . . well, I found Brodski, didn't I? If not for that pending referral, who knows where I'd be now . . . and he (though he's not the first playmate to come my way directly through office channels). But who would have thought when we started that the Department would protect me from spending my own money on him? It's not that I'm scrimping and saving here. As far as I'm concerned, there's no better way to spend my money. Oh, I admit I live my life prudently. I have no vices, no excesses, and I ravenously accumulate savings in my contingency fund. But there are limits. If I buy all the equipment I need to do him justice I'd have to be prepared for an outlay of thousands of dollars. This amount exceeds anything my contingency fund would permit by far. Luckily, (luck has little to do with it) I have calculated a way for the Department to assume the entire cost. It's really quite simple. And the money I save now will be put to good use later on. Either on Brodski or on someone like him. All that is necessary is to get Regina Dailey to order the equipment I need. A simple medical request form, W401, emanating from her office to the New York State Department of Health Sys-

75

tems and Management, and in a matter of weeks Brodski should have everything he needs.

Naturally I can't have her order all the equipment I need for a single client only. So I'll vary it. I'll have her order a utensil holder, which will allow Brodski to hold a paintbrush, pen or pencil (or all three at the same time), for Salvatore Domingo, a client of mine who by coincidence uses a similar contraption. No one will know that Domingo's own holder wasn't really lost. His caseworker says it was. That's enough. For another client, Antonio Morales, a spastic quadraplegic, I'll have her order a workplace desk or adjustable work table, which will serve as Brodski's easel. Even though his past medical history doesn't show any prior need for such equipment, Antonio is now ("miraculously") attending night school and studying computer training. He's the pride of my caseload. A letter from me, plus letters from his school administrator, a social worker at the Institute of Rehabilitation, and our own MSW, all testifying that his long hours of nightly study will be greatly facilitated by having such equipment, will be all that is necessary to establish this need. Even Mrs. Knox won't complain. Not when it's essential to the Department's long-range goal of making Antonio self-sufficient.

When the supplies arrive, I can pick them up at Antonio's home. We have an excellent working relationship. I've known him since he was a child and have never reported to the Social Security Administration that he's earning ("miraculously") extra money by working at his school in a part-time capacity. Also he selects his own Home Attendants (in certain situations clients are allowed to do this) and makes his own financial arrangements with them, which I've never interfered with. On the contrary, I've encouraged him; it does me good to witness such entrepreneurial spirit. I've even helped him along by documenting that the Home Attendants work for more hours than they do, thus increasing their paycheck. I do what I can to help. Sometimes one doesn't have to profit tangibly. To be thought of as a God, or even a benevolent despot, is enough.

Some items won't be so easy to procure. They'll require hours, perhaps days, of research on my part. There's not one client on my caseload, for instance, who I can honestly say has a need for a plate positioner (not for food but as a palette to hold paints and tubes for); or a safety bar kit, which will prevent Brodski from falling out of his chair. Thus I'll have to scrutinize my entire unit's cases as well as those of other co-workers on the floor. What I'll do is stay late in the office several nights and go through all the case records. Especially those referred to the Department by the Institute of Rehabilitation and Hospital for Special Surgery.

Also, I'll keep my ears open. B-25 this very morning mentioned that he has a client who uses a relaxation chair with nineteen different seating positions and seventy more for adjusting the upper body, and what's-his-name across the hallway in Unit K stated something about a youngster on his caseload using a magnetic wrist hold-down. I have never before appreciated just how fortunate I am that at least ninety percent of the cases here at Dept. 29 are composed of the elderly and infirm, or are referrals from SSI and Aid to the Disabled. In my unit alone there are half a dozen amputees who use artificial limbs. After I track down these clients, it'll just be a simple matter of going through the same procedure as before, with perhaps one or two minor variations. The actual caseworker doesn't even have to know. I can forge his signature as well as the client's on any necessary form. Even Regina Dailey is superfluous. I can forge her signature as well. And there's little risk in filling out the W401 form and submitting it in a brown manilla inter-office envelope either. I have all the forms and letterheads at my disposal, and given that, there's no limit to what a man of my imagination and resourcefulness can do. When the equipment is ready for delivery—and I'll know the date—I'll just call the client and say a mistake has been made, please accept the merchandise, and we'll have a man over to your house later this afternoon to cart it away.

Everything considered, I should have all of Brodski's

special equipment within six to eight weeks. The arm and hand prosthesis I will order through the Institute of Rehabilitation with the aid of Mrs. Thea Goldstein.

. . ."Why, Mr. Haberman, I think that's a wonderful idea. But why did you say we don't have to order leg prosthesis too?"

While I was waiting for the bus this morning the temperature dipped below five degrees. The wind was so fierce that neither fur, cloth, nor skin could shield against its unrelenting shivers. People on the way to the bus shelter were slipping and sliding on the frozen ice, and those who had already safely reached their destination were shrouded in their own solitary system of survival. Naturally, on this morning, the bus was late. Thirty minutes of refrigeration at the crosstown 66th Street bus stop. When the bus finally arrived, I alone was able to withstand temptation. While all the other men and women hastened to position themselves in place to gain entry, I stepped discreetly aside, and even went so far as to hold the pneumatic door with its hard rubber edge, while helping a woman with child aboard. I was all smiles; the perfect gentlemen. By imposing such discipline on myself now, I will be all the more ready to unleash myself on Brodski later.

Mother has gone away for the weekend of her own accord. I didn't even have to suggest her visiting her sister's home in Massachusetts twice. I did go "halfsies" with her. Though she paid for her friend, I paid for Mother. They left Friday afternoon. I started for home with Brodski (the first time he has stayed at my place for an entire weekend) the moment the checker cab took off. The last I saw of them they had turned in the direction of FDR Drive.

My studio apartment has all the features of an artist's garret now. Everything careless, lackadaisical and purposefully strewn about. The only thing missing is the proverbial skylight, but I do have bay windows and a park view. Still, Montparnasse it's not. There are canvases everywhere: rolls of canvas, stretched canvas, some stretched and mounted on canvas boards. Also a dozen paintbrushes, round and flat and long, and even more tubes of paint in all colors; Payne's gray, burnt sienna, burnt umber, viridian, sepia, zinc white, naples yellow, cobalt blue, yellow ochre, thalo green, venetian red. And an artist's smock and easel, and roto tray, and turntable, and palette. Everything and anything that goes into an artist's studio is here, plus all of Brodski's own special equipment.

The little fellow doesn't know what to make of it. He peers open-mouthed as I strap him to his artist's chair— the relaxation chair with nineteen different seating positions and seventy more for the upper body—and commence attaching his arm and hand prosthesis. The occupational therapist I employed has taught me well and I know how to use each piece of equipment as well as how to staple the stretched canvas tightly to the canvas board so

79

it won't ripple. When he is seated at his workplace (easel) with the canvas before him and rivulets of paint already squeezed out on his plate positioner (palette), I say: *PAINT.*

He looks at me, at the canvas, at his surrounding, dumbfounded. Not paralyzed, but stricken in another way. As if in limbo. As if groping to understand, to come to terms with what lies before him. I am tempted to help him. It would be such a simple matter for me to demonstrate how to "finger" the paintbrush with his table writer, or, for more exact control, his pencil holder; how to, with what for him would amount to a Promethean effort, touch the canvas with his brush. But I do not. It wouldn't be fair. The rules of the game do not permit it. The first stroke must be done by him. The discovery has to be his. The miracle must come from him alone. To be godlike, one has to create his own world. It is enough for me (now) to show him the way.

We sit there five, ten, twenty minutes; an hour passes, two. I do not say anything. Do not coax him on. Not so much as a word or hint passes from my lips. Absolute silence pervades the room. Then: he begins to move. Slowly at first, with imperceptible little stirrings of his body, followed by epileptic twitchings and wrigglings of his arms and hands. What's this? He's stretching-reaching-picking up the paintbrush lying on the plate positioner in a glass cup, just begging for his use. He's dipping it in a glob of paint. He's . . . He's . . . HE'S PAINTING!!! His first stroke is slow, halting, tenuous, as if a spanked child were reaching out for the object that caused him harm. He looks enthralled—no, terrified. After his first stroke he jerks back; his paint brush drops from his utensil holder against the glass cup and pan holding the other brushes and tubes of paint, and the entire collection as well as the roto tray spills to the floor. He doesn't even notice. Awestruck, he just continues to stare at the canvas. At a gashed slightly less than linear violet smudge: HE MADE!

A tiny wet spot wells up in his eye. A soft voluptuous half sigh, half groan, and then more tears, a sound that emanates from deep inside him, an indistinct murmur, a shriek, an ecstatic outcry, a crescendo of uncontrollable and involuntary body-racking shakes and sobs. He is crying. Really crying! Not his usual "cri du chat"; but crying like us. Like we humans do.

A half hour passes before he is able to start up again. This time by trial and error, each dip and dab of his brush reminiscent of a naked hand in a fire struggling to save a beloved object. After each new impression, he stops haltingly to examine it. Not for aesthetic reasons. He has no concern for that now. But for the sheer effect of it. The impression he is making on the canvas. ON THE WORLD! It is the first time he has ever been able to affect the world. Make his mark. HE IS PUTTING HIS STAMP ON THE WORLD!!!

After maybe another minute or two he falls back exhausted. I push his chair away from the canvas and together we look upon his creation. Grazing my hand ever so slightly on his utensil holder, as if touching the finger of God, I begin to cry. We begin to laugh and cry together. We stay there in tableau like that, both crying and laughing, the rest of the night.

. . . . I was in a bar having a drink to celebrate my recent victory. On the TV screen in the front were two fighters having a go at each other in the manly art of self-defense. The gladiators were drenched in blood; the grunts and groans of their pummeling efforts magnified a thousand decibels by the microphones the TV people had placed ringside. No one in the audience of tens of millions—not myself, the men loitering under the opalescent light of the bar, or even the acknowledged media experts—could detect where one man had the slightest advantage over the other. There was nothing to separate them. They were both equal. A man standing next to me, guzzling beer, by all appearances an ex-pug, said, "I don't know which one of these guys is ahead now or going to win it, but those guys in center ring know. One guy says, I got it. I'm going to win. The other guy knows he's a loser. It's a matter of

81

will. Nothing visible, nothing tangible, but it's there just the same. It happens every time."

The time is coming to bend Brodski's will. Submit it to mine. Up to now I've treated him with kid gloves. Partly because it was necessary to win his confidence. Partly to see what he could do. How high he could climb. But now he will have to be brought down from his pedestal. Yes: The time is fast approaching for Brodski to *FALL*.

In looking over these notes I find for the most part I have been referring to my encounters with Brodski as games up to now. And in a certain sense they are games to me. But my encounters will grow increasingly more serious from now on. Indeed, the further we go, the closer to the real thing they become. No longer are we playing games. Fun has ceased to be the sole means of keeping score.

One thing still bothered me: Was his artistic talent commensurate with his desire to paint? Any apprehension I had was soon overcome. Once he got used to the equipment and was able to accommodate himself to the necessary adjustment, he began painting in a frenzy. I witnessed such a gushing forth of creative energy I can only compare it to what I've heard tell and read of the great masters. It was as if he were making up for a lifetime's privation with each brush stroke. Everything he's seen and sees turns into a painting. Every part of him seems to create. He shows no preference for right or left artificial limb. Ambidextrous, he paints with both hands. Or more accurately, he paints with his soul. His entire being comes into play: body, mind, soul participate equally. All he is and has he gives to his work. On the average he paints two, three, maybe as many as four canvases a day, although sometimes he takes a week or longer to finish a larger, more ambitious project. I have seen him spend as much as a month on one painting; an entire day on a single feature of his composition. His concentration, like his energy level, is immense. He stays with a work in progress until it is right.

At first I thought he knew where he was going with each new work, but not really. Many times he'll just sit for hours staring with lusterless eyes at his canvas, and then, AHA! he perks up and starts again.

Nothing can detract him from his work. Chopin's military mazurka in F Minor can be playing, or I can allow the cacophony of vulgar street sounds to enter our studio by leaving the window open, but he goes on unperturbed. Even his heretofore favorite painting, a slide of Munch's The Scream, cannot deter him from his mission. When creating, his appreciation and interest in other men's work is null and void. He is like a writer who finds all the other books in the world a distraction when he is working on his own manuscript. Often he even paints with the lights out. In fact, he seems to prefer it that way. Closer to his imagination, I guess. Nor does he eat anything but the most meager breakfast all day. First, because he so eagerly awaits my arrival to take him to the studio (Mother still thinks we go for walks outside), and then, when he's there, because there's no stopping him: he can't wait to get at his own canvas. He attacks it voraciously. He has no need of anything except to paint. Nothing else exists for him.

In such a way are masterpieces made?

I spend each afternoon observing him. He is as indifferent to me as to everything else. Once he begins to paint, he goes into a trance, curling his white-coated tongue over his chinless chin. He is happy, I'm certain. Who has ever been so happy? So full, rich and complete? I envy him during these hours. I hate him. The more he becomes one with his art, the more I come to realize what real work might have meant in my life. Each new inspiration of his only further widens the chasm between me and my own tawdry, humdrum work. I gaze in unblinking awe at each stroke of his brush as if he were a great master and I his student and to miss one would be the same as to miss life's most important lesson.

In fact, so taken am I by Brodski that ever since meeting him, and especially since discovering he's an artist, I have been regularly spending ten to twenty hours a week in the public library doing homework on him. Reading books on art history and method, the question of talent vs. genius, the cat cry syndrome, and on the aforementioned so-called Great Masters. Of course, I read this material in my own way. You won't find any respect bordering on reverence inside of me. The experience of art is not like entering a cathedral for me. Nor do I have any naive expectation that art can effect a profound change within me. Even if I did all the research in the world, would it enable me to paint one good picture? Create a single masterpiece? Nor is cultivation my goal; nor appreciation; nor love of knowledge. Maybe least of all love of knowledge. Nor do I have a college boy's inclination to indulge myself in idle theories on aesthetics, or wild masturbatory speculations on art. And even if I did, with whom would I do so? Mrs. Knox? Brodski? No. My purposes today (always) are pragmatic. Utilitarian. "Be prepared" is my motto. "Know who the enemy is." And so like a West Point cadet who fancies himself a future general, I consume these pages like the battle plans and stratagems and stockpile of military information they really are.

But even with all this knowledge and assiduous preparation I don't delude myself for a second that I will ever be able to enter Brodski's head completely. When all is said and done, I am as alone as he is. Perhaps the best I can hope for is for us to be alone together. For that I must be able to make educated guesses as to what his paintings mean. With this intent and purpose I have begun naming them; labeling them; or, should I say, reducing them to size? It is quite apparent to me that the more I use my own words and vocabulary to interpret his work, the more I might be straying from their original meaning. But what else can I do? He won't tell me any more than I already know, and at least this way I can make some sense out of them for *My Own Purposes.*

84

And even if his work does remain beyond my grasp, describing his different techniques is well within reach. And although his approach altogether might be called Abstract Impressionism, one technique in particular—his Primitive Minimalist technique—deserves special mention. He starts out flushing all the color and oil on the canvas he can. Saturating its surface to excess. Then instead of adding, he subtracts. From the luscious thick oil of his initial outpouring, his surface gets progressively thinner as the subject he works on becomes more and more precise. With time there comes a certain austerity. By amputating those features of his composition that seem to him superfluous (and to us, essential) he attains his vision of reality. A vision so pure you can see it all at once. His paintings at the end strike me as luminous, fundamental. By their very scarcity and lack are they complete and whole. Knowing the world as it is today and looking at his paintings—and at him—I ask myself: Could he be right? Is less more?

He looks as if he has more fun than other artists if only because he is more preoccupied with taking away than adding to. On his face he wears an absurd, silly glued-on smile. In spite of the abstract quality and spareseness of his canvas there are always a few things sprinkled throughout that strike me as social comment. They are the key; they unravel the mystery for me. Usually his images are taken from real life. A particular favorite of mine is his version of Mother and Child. At least, I call it that. The way I see it, he has the mother typically cradling the babe in her arms with the child's lips outstretched and groping for the nipple. But he cannot reach it. The mother is turned away, immersed in another task. It leaves you with the succinct impression: Will the babe ever reach his goal?

All in all, he plays no favorites. All the great subjects—good, evil, God, love, right, wrong, sin, guilt—draw his attention equally. There is no doubt his work has merit. Forget all the books. One glance at any of his final compositions tells you that.

By the end of the day he has nothing left. He collapses in his chair, having used up his last drop of energy with the last stroke of his brush. He is literally in a daze as I carry him home. Only then will he eat and allow his other needs

85

to be attended to. Following supper, for example, he delights in a warm bath. Having soaked for an hour, reveling in his joy, he is ready to sleep with the angels. And, wrinkled as a fetus, I put him to bed. Oh yes, one last thing. His erections are stronger than ever now. Eros, I concur with the Neo-Freudians, definitely has something to do with more than one kind of creation.

After leaving him, I prefer to walk home rather than take a bus or subway. It gives me a chance to unwind for the day. During these brisk wintry night walks my mind conjures up images of the next phase of our relationship. The last phase. Like Brodski, I have things to look forward to, though I don't sleep as well as he does these nights. My obsessions won't let me.

THE FALL BEGINS: Laden with gifts, I rushed into Brodski's apartment at noontime today. Mother and son had not seen me in such a tether for a long time. Mother had already bundled Brodski up and he was ready to leave for the studio to paint. But we never left. Instead I hurried into his room, unwrapped my lavishly giftwrapped presents, and took down from the wall three of his favorite prints. In their place I hung three paintings of his own. They were simply but elegantly framed; each frame wonderfully suited to the particular painting. Then I centered them and adjusted the dimmer lights. When I finished, Mother exclaimed that these "pictures" were even more beautiful than the ones that previously hung there. Bordski didn't utter a word. At first he seemed confused, then happy. My guess is that it was not only seeing his beautiful paintings that made him happy. His happiness had more to do with the only real interest an artist can have in such things: the pride and joy of having *made* them. As he continued to gaze upon his paintings, I slipped out the door undetected by him, signaling Mother to join me. I asked her to care for Brodski that afternoon because I could not. "I have something more important to do."

Her ambivalence manifested itself at once. That the prospect of spending an entire afternoon with her son once again had a certain appeal there was no denying; but she had purchased a week ago two tickets for a Latin music festival to attend with her friend at Madison Square Garden that very day, and that prospect also had a certain hold. So she stood betwixt and between, unable to decide. There was no doubt in my mind that it was up to me to help her. And I did. After rummaging through my suit pockets, I calmly removed two tickets for the same concert

87

for the following Wednesday afternoon and I gave them to her gratis. To make my offer even more attractive, I volunteered to reimburse her for her own two tickets, which were nonreturnable because she had bought them at a special discount price. The fact that my tickets were floor level and hers balcony, I must confess, came as a complete surprise to me, although, of course, it didn't hurt my bargaining position any. Still, in all fairness to Mother, I think that at this particular moment she was more interested in being with her son again than in any fiduciary gain. In any event, my negotiations successfully completed, I left at once.

Now, only when I'm gone, will Brodski come to understand that he won't paint today. It is good that the discovery comes while I'm not there. It will be all the more poignant and telling that way. The last he saw of me I bore presents and was scrupulously hanging his paintings to the exact centimeter required. Now a thousand contradictory thoughts enter his head, and some painful doubts. He doesn't know what to make of me. In the most important way I have let him down. He has only Mother and his paintings to spend the afternoon with. How could I do this to him? Be so insensitive? Not know that they are not enough? Not realize that a finished work, even his own, can never compare to one in progress or yet to be made? It is only the next work, the new creation, that is of real value to the artist: I, of all people, must know that. The ones already finished, hanging on the walls like dead things, are just that: dead. After a half hour he will hardly be able to bear looking at them any longer. He will want to paint. Mother won't have the faintest idea what's bothering him. "You have your new paintings, darling, the ones Mr. Haberman was kind enough to bring over for you. Why are you. . . ?" And a half hour later: "For this I had to stay home and miss my con . . . Spoiled brat! Selfish!" THE FALL HAS BEGUN!!!

"It's not fair!" says Mother Earth.

"Why should our Department be picked on!" says Rodent Face.

"Why not the policemen! The hospital workers! The transit workers! The teachers! The firemen! The clerical workers! say A-21, B-22, C-25, D-24, E-26, and F-23.

The Secretary-treasurer of local 371—an oral fixed type if ever there was one, he can speak for interminable stretches of time about nothing—has just completed his warning speech on *City layoffs!* "No use kidding ourselves," he said. "The rumors are true. Be prepared for it. We're next. You know how the Mayor has always hated this Department. The cops and the firemen are his favorites. Even the garbagemen rank ahead of us in his opinion." Now is the time for questions and answers. And the workers don't disappoint him. They attack in full fury . . . The very same people who only days before were voicing their displeasure with *"How much I hate this job . . . I'll never stay . . . First chance I get, I'm leaving . . . Gone!* now vocalize with the same fervor their indignation about being sacrificial lambs at the mercy of the Mayor! City Hall! Downtown! City, state and federal purse strings! Corrupt city officials! Previous administrations! Etc., etc. The Secretary-treasurer's insatiable need for oral gratification is satisfied beyond all expectations.

His meeting scheduled for the waking hours of the morning, between 9:30 a.m. and 11:00 a.m. continued on until 3:45 in the afternoon. Worthy civil servants, many coming from as far off as Brooklyn, the Bronx and Queens to hear their mighty union oracle, populate our fifth-floor office, which is now filled to brimming with more faces than I've ever seen here. One of the great staples of the world, lunch, is dispensed with. No one has the stomach for it. Not even Mother Earth (fried chicken and chocolate cake) and Rodent Face (liverwurst on rye), whose lunch habits heretofore have always been as constant as Mrs. Knox's clarion call for statistics at the end of the month. Everyone is absolutely aghast at the great oracle's prophecy. And why shouldn't they be? Their entire civil service life-plan freighted with all those wonderful benefits—pension plan, hospital plan, medical plan, annual leave, sick leave, coffee break, and no one harassing them, competing against them for their job, their money, their raises—all those hard-won freebies and fringe benefits will be so much water under the bridge now if they're laid off.

Even I stayed to listen. Not so much because I was interested in what the union delegate had to say (deep down I don't feel anything pertaining to the job has anything to do with me): it was just that I felt it an excellent opportunity to pique my colleagues. When people are at their lowest, I seem to rise to the occasion. I'm at my best in those dour moments and can often, without hardly trying, display a satirist's gift for wit and humor. And from the moment the Secretary-treasurer opened his mouth that morning, I knew the opportunity was there to outdo myself:

"Colleagues and co-workers, our Secretary-treasurer is right. If we have any legitimate grievances, let's form a committee, organize our thoughts, write them on paper, and submit them per procedure 18-787 to his office at once."

"The hell with procedures! We want our jobs!!!"

"Fellow workers, when you signed up with the Department and attained civil service status you attained more than words. You attained a lifelong contract with the City of New York, and I quote: *'You are insured a job for life.'* Could we ask for anything more from this great city of ours?!"

"But I have the least seniority of the whole staff here. If the layoffs come, I'll be the first to go."

"Only so a favored city official downtown can support his mistress in the style she is accustomed to, my man."

"And what about my wife and kids? She's sickly, needs some kind of female operation, and those darn kids all got buck teeth. Who's going to pay for their braces?"

"My dear man, ugliness builds character. We all know that. And as for your wife, women can survive anything. They're the stronger sex. Just ask them. Besides, in today's world, who honors contracts? And even if you are civil service and your job is for life, that doesn't mean they can't take it away from you. In fact, this only proves they can!"

And so I heckled, incited, rabble-roused not merely my colleagues in Unit B and from the other units, but my peers and cohorts who joined us from the other four boroughs as well. I doubt sincerely if even Brodski could have brought me such unadulterated joy. It made up for a goodly portion of my thirty-four years' association with the Department.

It goes without saying that my missed visits with Brodski didn't do any harm either. Why should he be exempt from life's vicissitudes? On the contrary, it fits right in with all the plans I have in store for him in the weeks and months ahead.

Since that day two weeks ago when the Secretary-treasurer spoke to us about the inevitability of layoffs much has happened in the Department. Tonita, our two-hundred-and-fifty pound clerk-typist hippo, has gone off her rocker and called in the police. Something about the Director spying on her. Bugging her telephone calls. A simple case of too much pressure. Perhaps she shouldn't have written on the grievance sheet submitted to the union delegate's office in triplicate, per procedure 18-787, that the Director's horticultural interests were the main reason why the Mayor hates our Department so. She was suspended this past Monday.

And Richard Gould has become fanatical about his W712 field-visit recording form. He goes over it after work every day now. Why after work? Because he doesn't have time during normal working hours. He's too busy racing around in the field or filling out other forms in the office. Of course, he's going back to when he first joined our unit. Not an easy task when you consider that takes in two and one-half years. That's a lot of field time to go over. Especially for a man who has never missed making a visit in his life.

As for our Office Liason, Hans Becker, nothing bothers him. He's been down this route before. But then, why did he cancel his art show . . . voluntarily?

Mrs. Knox? Merely more grist for her statistical mill. "Now everybody will tow the line," she says, "or else!" As her first priority she called for a complete review of all case record entries. "Some are illegible, others merely not written neatly enough. They will have to be written over."

"All of them, Mrs. Knox?" I ask. "Some of my caseload dates back years."

"All of them, Mr. Haberman, and yours in particular. Your handwriting is atrocious. I'm probably the only person in the entire office who can make it out."

"He probably wants it that way," mumbles Richard Gould. "He makes up all his visits. If you can't read them, how are you going to verify anything he says or whether he's been there or not?"

I don't argue with my Supervisor. (Or Richard Gould). The fact is, I agree with her. Downtown means business. For the next several weeks and more, much more, I plan on staying in the office the better part of the afternoon to review and, if necessary, rewrite each and every one of my case record entries. Despite my bold words, and even if I do have seniority, one can never be too safe in times like these. I have enemies in the Department. Mrs. Knox, for example, after fifteen years would like nothing better than to get rid of me. And then, the other workers will take more kindly to me, seeing me work so hard. Besides, my handwriting is atrocious.

There are other things I can do to ingratiate myself with Mrs. Knox and the others. From now on when Mrs. Knox's daughter calls I'll make a special effort to be cordial with her. To take her messages courteously. That's not as easy as it sounds when you consider she's a duplicate of her mother. And in the mornings when my supervisor and colleagues babble on about office gossip, or what they ate last night or watched on TV, or the day's headlines, or some celebrity who's caught their fancy for an hour, I'll listen politely. No longer will I exhibit smug aloofness. In fact, I'll join in. I'll respond with blandishments. Again it won't be easy . . . but it shouldn't be too difficult. These sessions only last ten to fifteen minutes. By 9:15 things are back to normal: The workers are buried in their death routine, the hate has surfaced, the day has begun.

I thank Providence that Brodski is in his final phase. This enforced unresponsiveness to his creative needs happens to coincide with my plans for him. One must always look for the good things, I repeat to myself over and over as I rewrite my past case record entries one at a time.

"Staying in late again, Mr. Haberman?"

"Yes, Mrs. Sampson. It seems these days I can't get enough of you."

. . . . Coming home from work today on the subway, between the 96th Street and the 72nd Street stop, I saw a beautiful young woman. Besides makeup (an excessive amount), teased hair and a faraway look (she refused to acknowledge my stare), she had a withered left arm. It was more like a fin than a normal arm. Two forked fingers jutted out from a paper-thin stem that was adorned by a thin gold bracelet.

Before getting off, I pushed past several other passengers to ask her where she bought the bracelet.

I have been going over these case record entries for what seems like forever now; two weeks straight, till 5:00p.m.

93

each day; over and over and over again. My head feels as if it's wedged between a case record vise. I have what must be writer's cramp in my hand. If I never look at another case record again the rest of my life, it will be too soon. Going to sleep at night, all I see are case record W2 entry sheets with their marginal headings: Problem. Family Composition. Eligibility for Services. Health. Relatives. Living Conditions. Service Plan. Recommendation. On and on and on. Again and again and again. Every marginal heading means another rewrite and another and another. Whenever I take a break for five minutes, not leaving my desk, just looking around the office at my fellow workers expending pretty much the same nose-to-the-grindstone energies on similar efforts, one thing alone sustains me: Brodski. The little fellow has not touched a brush now for an even longer period of time than I have been writing these !?*%$! case record entries. He must be as famished for creation as a starving man is hungry for food. Good. That is the way I want him. When I get out, and I will, he will . . . That is the day we both await.

In the meantime, enough frivolous talk, wishful thinking. Back to work. Marginal heading: Problem. Family Composition. Eligibility for Services. Health. Relatives. Living Conditions. Service Plan. Recommendation. On and on and on. Again and again and again.

Pardon my broken record, but that's just the way I feel. I'm tipsy from overwork, boredom, physical and mental fatigue. I hate this job, myself, Brodski. I will get out. He will . . .

It was difficult for me to interpret his reaction when seeing him for the first time in so long. Perhaps it is enough to describe him. He was haggard, drawn; a benign grey beard sprouted straggly on his chin; he smelled badly. Mother had ignored him for the most part, begrudging him her maternal labors, and understandably so. No matter what she did for him, she said, no matter how hard she tried, his mood never changed. He remained dismal and glum "when you aren't here." And now that I am—is he happy? Does he envision at least a faint hope on the horizon? I think so. But even I cannot be certain. What I do know is that his dull gaze and absence of zeal left him the moment I arrived. And when I shaved him and scrubbed him spotless he was restless as if he wanted to go somewhere. To the studio? Then say so, darling. You know the word. S-T-U-D-I-O. Here, after me, like this. S-T-U-D-I-O.

To add to his frustration, I insisted he eat breakfast before we departed. Mother said he hadn't touched a bite (and she's not one to exaggerate) since that last day I called informing her about the emergency in the office that would prevent me from taking him out on our daily strolls for the next several weeks. Only after he had gulped down his last mouthful and I was satisfied that he had something substantial in his tummy did I rush him off to the studio to paint.

It is a good day for creation. The season is changing from winter to spring. There are colors burgeoning about everywhere. A patch of blue in the sky; a mat of green in the park. There, look! A young woman bedecked in a coat of many colors across the street. (He didn't notice). Colors to paint with, my dear. To liven up the old bloodstream. You are alive once again.

Once at the studio, in his chair, with his arm and hand prostheses attached and his easel and canvas before him, he burst into tears. But these are easy tears to interpret. They are happy tears. He is happy. After every few strokes he makes, I adjust the angle on his relaxation chair; because there are so many different positions for seating, and even more for moving the upper body, I have what is almost an infinity of combinations and permutations to play with. At first Brodski hardly noticed. He was so happy to once again be at his labor of love that he probably thought I was only trying to make him more comfortable so he could paint better. After a while, though, when I changed the angles more sharply and it became increasingly evident that I wasn't out to help him—on the contrary, quite the reverse—I heard an occasional cry or muffled whimper come from him. But they were restrained, as though he was afraid to express what he really had in mind. By the end of the hour the angles I was experimenting with were so acute that no matter how he adjusted his magnetic wrist hold-down, or manipulated his universally adjustable hand-splint, he could barely reach the canvas with his brush.

All his plaintive grievances, which had increased considerably, were to no avail. I continued to change the positions each time I thought he was making the least bit of progress in adapting to them. After a certain point—precisely two and one half hours from the time we started, on his twelfth seating position, to be exact (I, too, keep records), and his thirty-ninth for the upper body—his fits and tantrums stopped and not another sound was heard from him. It was as if he had decided to brave it from that time on. Artists have endured more for the sake of their art, so why not he? Besides, it's better than being at home having to listen to Mother's chronic laments, isn't it, little one? At least here there's something to be gained. A worthy cause. Compared to Mother, these little orbital spins of mine must seem as exciting as soaring in space—upside down, topsy turvy, at a 180-degree angle lying flat on his tummy suspended in midair like Cupid aiming his arrow.

Nothing stops him from painting though. As difficult as it was for the little fellow, one thing I'll grant him. He never compromised a stroke. He never shirked his duty. If he didn't hit it right the first time, or the second, or the eighteenth, he just started again. He'd dab his brush in the paint-remover varnish—this was a painstaking procedure for him—and go on from there. He endured all my space-spinning explorations as if they were just so many penances he had to pay to be a member of his holy artistic order.

Was it worth it? As they say, depends on how you look at it . . . or who looks at it. When I took him home at the end of the day he was so dispirited he couldn't even eat or avail himself of his nice warm bath and accompanying genital message (first time he ever missed that). But I'm certain that because of the difficulties I put him through which made him exercise his concentration to the fullest, he did produce good work.

Very different from my own work progress I'm sure. No matter how many times I write and rewrite this dribble, Mrs. Knox still finds something wrong. My handwriting is still atrocious. And she's right. That's not to say I don't suffer as much as Brodski in my work. I do. But evidently suffering isn't the only prerequisite for producing good work. Perhaps one must suffer in a special way.

What way?

I expect that Brodski will show me.

I have cast Mother aside for good. From now on Brodski stays with me and Mother will be permitted to visit my modest bachelor quarters only by appointment. Little did she understand the ramifications of my offer last week to treat her for the Easter vacation to a fully paid return trip to "her country," Puerto Rico. I just gave her the Eastern Airline tickets, Flight number 179 ($197.20), as well as spending money, three hours ago. Away with you! Begone! May you have the worst flight possible and I read about you in the morning headlines: Eastern Airline DC-10 Jet Liner Crashes Killing . . . As usual, Mother took her friend with her, though this time I had to pay her way too. Mother refused to treat her and the woman had already expended almost her entire life savings on making a down payment for a home in her native land. It seems both women came from the same little village, Old San Juan, and shared the same dream to return to it at some time in their lives together before it was too late. But, of course, they never did. It took me to make it happen. When it comes right down to it—money!—Mother is as tight fisted as any of us. The more she has, the more she wants. She hardly parts with a nickel nowadays if she can help it. And why should she? Did we not come to a tacit agreement over a month ago that I would act as her rich uncle in return for certain favors?

Now I have Brodski all to myself. The arrangements I made with Mother were "temporary," until she gets back from her Easter vacation; when, she thinks, I also have to return to work. But I know better, don't I? At that time I'll tell her I've taken a leave of absence from my job and Brodski simply doesn't want to go home with her. One look at him then and she'll have to agree. And the truth is he never will go back to her now regardless of how I treat him; not when he's actually within "sitting distance" of his beloved canvas, and when his painting is dependent upon pleasing me. Mother's ambivalence and ensuing guilt will be easy to appease. Her greed and cumulative months of frustration with Brodski will far outweigh any tender feelings she still might have for him. Also, per our tacit alliance, a few more dollars in the till won't hurt either. And she won't have to drink alone at night. Oh, didn't I mention it? Mother has taken to sousing it up lately. The negative influence of her friend, a rummy, as well as, perhaps, some deeper, more personal problems.

I've made arrangements with Caesar Rosario, my client, Antonio Morales' Home Attendant, to care for Brodski during my working hours. I told him that after he leaves Antonio's house at 8:00 in the morning (that's when Antonio leaves for school) he can just as well come over to my apartment for his morning nap. Brodski will have already been cleaned, talcumed, diapered, and eaten his breakfast by that time, and other than changing his bed position once or twice, Caesar shouldn't have anything to do until I return home at noontime to care for him the rest of the day.

"Yes, Caesar, the Department doesn't have to know anything about the money you earn. In fact, I prefer it that way. That's why I'll be paying you cash on the line personally. What do you mean can you trust me? Who do you think's been Antonio's caseworker all these years!? . . . Oh, Caesar before you leave, one last thing. My art studio. . . . Yes, Caesar, I do a lot of painting. Painting's the love of my life. You're not into it. Into women. Well, each to his own, as they say. Anyway, no matter. Just make certain you don't touch a thing."

Mother put up more of a fight than I had anticipated. Apparently mixing with the natives regenerated her ancient maternal instinct. And learning that I had transplanted all of Brodski's belongings during her absence—dresser, crib-bed, art objects, prints, everything; his room here is a virtual replica of his room at Mother's apartment, only the view is different, and in some respects better—I imagine didn't do her any good either. But as I thought he would be all along, Brodski was the clincher. The little fellow would have nothing to do with her when she came to visit us this afternoon upon her return from the hinterlands. One look from me when she tried to remove one of his figurines from the dresser and he let out such a shriek of protest that he literally drove her home in tears. I can just see Mother taking a few extra quaffs this evening with her friend.

Maybe I ought to send them a bottle of champagne.

On second thought, I'd better not. My contingency fund's not all it used to be and there's really no sense overdoing it.

How can I say what it's like having Brodski as my roommate? I can do anything I want with him. He no longer has Mother to protect him. Not that she did such a good job of it or ever interfered with me, but just her mere presence was sufficient to dampen my spirits. She could be sitting silently staring vacantly at the four walls (a favorite pastime of hers) and I took it as the foulest intrusion. Ask any unhappily married man what I mean: "My wife doesn't have to say a thing, just her being there, in the next room, is enough to spoil everything. Once we set up house it was all over. I could no longer be one of the boys, much less myself."

Once again I have absolute dominion over my life and what is the same thing: over Brodski. Morning, noon, afternoon and night I can give my wildest impulses free rein. I can take his favorite painting, Munch's The Scream, off the wall, mark it up, cut it up, in front of his eyes, and what can he do to stop me? I can do the same thing with any of his other prints or objets d'art, or even his own paintings. Whatever whim comes to me at the moment, no matter how fickle, I can translate into action. I can toss each love object of his, one by one, out the window, or if I prefer, if it so suits me, I can crumble, tear and shatter all of them into a thousand pieces, into tiny multicolored ribbons and fragments, and then toss the whole kit and kaboodle out of the window like so much confetti at a parade, and all he can do is sit there looking on. Or I can use his prints or paintings or his work in progress to cover my floors, as my grandmother used to do with old newspapers; I can trample upon them with dirty shoes when I return home after an April shower, or I can rip them to shreds with my iron-heeled boots, and what can he do to stop me!

I ASK YOU, LITTLE ONE: WHEN I AM DOING MY WORK AND YOU ARE WATCHING ME, WHO IS IT WHO'S MOST ALIVE THEN!?!

This morning I got up before dawn. I lifted Brodski from his crib-bed and took him to the rooftop and together we waited for the sunrise. When he saw the orange-red haze transform itself into the golden globe, his face dazzled the colors of the rainbow. Sitting there with him in my arms, crumpled up within himself like a turtle inside its shell, I knew he understood that nature's art was in every way superior to anything man-made.

I do the same at sunset. The demise of the day and the moon's quicksilver smile are equally beautiful to behold. My darling's sweet celestial purring sounds show me he is in complete accord.

Now every morning and night the little devil won't let me be. At sunrise and sunset my humble bachelor quarters echo with such crescendoes of sound that I have to wonder what the neighbors think. And coming from such a tiny body. He commences his wail to awaken me at the earliest hour, but if I rise, it is only to shut my bedroom door. I don't take him to the rooftop. At sunset I am likewise unavailable. I've gotten in the habit lately of taking my daily constitutionals at just that time. Besides my eight hours sleep I need my share of exercise these days to keep up. God knows I don't get it at the office. Though I don't jog. I think people jogging, especially women, are ugly.

Before leaving the office today I must remember to call an insulation company and make an appointment for them to send a man out to assess the cost of a complete soundproofing of my apartment.

The black woman who serves me my tuna fish on whole-wheat sandwich with hot chocolate every morning at the diner on 125th Street has one salient feature. It is not her vibrant, always cheerful voice, her frenetic all-hands energy, not even the extraordinary patience she exhibits with the glum-faced working people, the sleepy-eyed welfare recipients, or the gang of young punks who frequent her establishment regularly. It is her rear end. Her glutius maximus. Her pathetic efforts to squeeze these massive hams into shape with a panty girdle only magnifies how disgusting they are. For the past week and a half I have taken Broadski out to breakfast every morning.

"Oh, hi Caesar, thanks for coming over to pick him up. Want to join us for breakfast? . . . No, not at the table, Caesar. Here, at the counter. Alice can't see us over there, and we can't see her. And it's too early in the morning for me to be bouncing up and down out of my chair to get an order, and I'll be damned if Brodski's in any shape to serve as waiter.

". . . What you say? Why isn't he eating? He did already at home. You don't really expect him to have an appetite in a place like this, do you?

". . . Then why do I bring him here? Caesar, did it ever occur to you I might get lonesome eating here all by myself every morning?"

Forget caserecords. Forget work. As far as Brodski's concerned, things couldn't be better. I even have the weather on my side. It's so nice lately I've been taking him outdoors with me again virtually every day for the past several weeks. Only our sightseeing tours aren't what they used to be. No longer do I follow him. I lead the way. Brodski sees only what I want him to. As far as seeing anything beautiful, he might as well have blinders on for all the good it will do him to stretch that dradle neck of his. This past week alone I must have shown him more of the "real world" than he'd seen up to now even if you multiplied all our prior outings a hundred times over. And, yes: it's getting nicer out each passing day.

On Monday I stood over him in his carrying bag and made him watch a mental patient probably released from a nearby hospital forage through half a dozen different trash cans for scraps of food for at least two hours.

On Tuesday, coincidentally the same mental patient, only this time wandering through the city traffic in a dazed condition. We followed her for blocks until she fell, then we just stood there watching (I stood, he watched) her slobber over herself in an epileptic fit until an ambulence came and took her away.

On Wednesday, a bag lady with feet and legs swollen the size of an elephant's; a disheveled beggar man sunning himself on a park bench sheathed in tattered sheets, sweaters, shirts, and, to top it off, a shredded inside-out overcoat. It must have reached eighty-five degrees that day if it was one. And just before entering my building, I stopped before what I thought would be a real eye-catcher, the elliptical buzz-saw of flies feasting off dog excrement on my stoop. Imagine my surprise when Brodski wasn't upset by this. I waited and waited and gave him a good long look

102

but the little bastard refused to become unsettled. In the apartment I tried to make up for it by giving him another close-up, this time of his own feces, but again he showed no reaction. If anything, he appeared interested. I must be on guard not to bring in my own set of values here.

On Thursday we didn't go out. I didn't feel like it. But on Friday I made up for it and then some. A three-legged dog. That's right. You heard me. A three-legged dog. The woman standing beside us, upon seeing the scarred-up mongrel sniff and put his muzzle underneath her companion's skirt before continuing to hop, skip and jump along, murmured, "That's sad." She offered no such words of compassion for his owner (or Brodski). You won't believe this: his owner is also a cripple, also missing one leg. Brodski and I followed the four-legged (in toto) pair all the way to the cripple's home that day. You can be certain by the way Brodski reacted that sometime in the near future he's in for an encore.

On Saturday nothing so interesting. The best I could do was a handsome black youth on crutches. Quite accidentally turning my head diagonally to the left, I noticed a lumpy intersection of scars on his right hand. My first thought was that the surgeon had botched up the job. Not enough incentive, I figured. The youth and family (if there was a family) probably had no money. Let the interns work: Doc's out at the country club playing golf. In any event, since the day afforded me no better sight, I positioned Brodski in his carrying bag and made certain he got the same close-up of the disfigured hand I had.

As an added bonus I make certain that our excursions coincide directly with his preferred work hours. Not only do they come at the very time he is most habituated to painting, but seemingly on the spur of the moment. That way I know there's nothing he can do to prepare himself for them.

For example, I might return home at noon, dismiss the Home Attendant, and set Brodski at his easel and canvas so that he is bursting to paint. Or maybe he's already made his first stroke or laid his initial outpouring of oil and color on the canvas, or even well into the actual composition. It's only then that I permit the impulse to hit me. Or I remember something I don't know how in the world I forgot in the first place. Like having to make a seventy-two-hour pending visit (we have seventy-two hours from the time we get a new case to make initial contact; failure to comply and it's grounds for dismissal according to Mrs. Knox); or having promised to visit Harry Harris (I've been his caseworker for years and they're carting him off to a nursing home tomorrow; he's 101 years old and looks it) or Margaret Fenderson (my black-is-beautiful scorched-pinky-white-flesh fire victim case); or Carlin or Montero or Alice Miller or . . . Or perhaps the weather is so beautiful I decide it's just too nice to stay indoors: "Let's get some sunshine, darling. You can always paint later, So what if you're in the midst of an inspiration." Or: "Let's go for a walk in the rain." A French girl told me once she loved to walk in the rain. I thought she was daffy (still do), but maybe Brodski can see its merit. "It's only a spring shower, darling. It won't last long." Just long enough.

Always when he's most engrossed in his work does the impulse grab me or do I remember something. At those times I literally tear Brodski away from his beloved canvas and carry him off to see the pleasure pains of the world.

When we return home and he's shattered and ruined by the sights he's just seen, I try to make up for it by allowing him to paint. I permit him no respite. No rest period. No good night's sleep to refresh the system, or stiff drink to ease the burden of memory. The hurt and pain are still heavy inside him; the afterglow of the counter girl's disgusting fat ass, the intersection of scars on the handsome youth's hand, the three-legged dog hopping, skipping and jumping along with its one-legged master: they're all there, embedded in every painful pore of his body when I give him the order to: PAINT! Now or never, you little bastard . . . paint! What does he do? I give you one guess. You're wrong. He can't! The tears slowly slide down his misshapen face, to land on his receding chin, then roll up and over, like a waterfall that won't stop for any obstacle. I

104

let him absorb the full weight of his creative block before carrying him off to the bathroom.

You can bet he has no erections on those nights!

Even at work I manage to have fun these days. The office continues to have every appearance of a mausoleum as I gaze around the room looking for a worthy target to relieve my monotony. And there she is: Ms. Pais. My office favorite. In the pinch she's always good for a few laughs. Though she now sits apart from her unit, from the entire office staff—she was allotted a lone corner with a desk to herself after her last blowup—technically she's still considered a member of the department's family. Ms. Pais reads books all day long. Assiduously takes notes. No scholar in any of the great libraries of the world works harder than Ms. Pais. You can look up any time of the day and see her writing something down. Presumably for her night school course requirements toward getting a degree in accounting or business administration. Ms. Pais wants to improve her pocketbook if not her mind. Makes sense, doesn't it? Sure. But what doesn't make sense is that Ms. Pais hasn't passed one course in eleven years. Not one. If only you could see her. The fleshy parts of her underthighs lopping out of her dress one foot too short, the penguin straddle, the shrill high-pitched West Indian nasal sounds. Constant mutterings to herself. An absolute mess. Before retiring to bed this evening, being in such generous spirits thanks to Brodski, I decided to share my good cheer with my coworkers first thing in the morning.

Without anyone knowing it, I slink into the office before the other workers arrive and swipe one of Ms. Pais' tattered and well-marked books from her desk and naughtily slip it on a fellow worker's. I hate to describe what happened an hour later when Ms. Pais found that poor worker who unwittingly had her book on his desk. Suffice to say all hell broke loose. (If one can describe a catatonic fit in semireligious terms). What good ten thousand miligrams of

Valium against Ms. Pais' wrath. Not much. Just ask that poor worker—if you can find him. He took off for the field in the middle of an office emergency. It took two hours at least for Ms. Pais to calm down. But, alas, I might as well have been trying to cheer pallbearers riding a funeral hearse for all the success my efforts had on my fellow workers. They preferred to stay on their Sisyphus treadmill as if nothing was happening during those two hours from 9 to 11. They completely ignored Ms. Pais and did (not feigned, but did) a full morning's work. In fact, if anything, they exceeded their usual output. Such discipline, such good work habits, and "they" say civil servants use the least excuse not to work. Well, here's one who begs to differ. If the Ms. Pais incident is a precedent—and it is—I will vouchsafe they don't.

Not what's going on here? The little bastard's up to something. When I yanked him away from his canvas today while he seemed to be at a high point of creative activity, there was none of the usual show of protest on his part. He didn't as much as let out a whimper. If I didn't know better, I'd say he was almost happy. Grateful. He acted as if he was looking forward to it. Normally his hearing is so acute (like all his senses: taste, smell, touch; they compensate for his general condition) that even when I sneak up on him from behind when he has totally surrendered himself to his painting, somehow he knows I'm coming to interrupt him and he lets out a tremolo. It's his way of saying no. Today, if I'm honest with myself, by the very absence of that sound, he said yes! And then, when I took him with me on my visit to Mr. Bohatir and his vegetable-wife, he didn't act the least bit disturbed when I positioned him (he was in his wheelchair) in front of her bed. Her Home Attendant was working her over at the time and Brodski couldn't help but get a look at that diaphanous corpse-like body being lifted, pushed, shoved, and dropped into place. She was lying there as always, with

106

that huge water-in-the-skull and misshapen snaggle-toothed mouth of hers, not sad, not happy, but frozen in a gaping grimace of bedazed wonder. What eternal question was she pondering, if she could ponder? Yellow lines of urine trickled down her infant chubby thighs and brown stains smeared her stretched-marked rump and the small rectangular dry-down underneath her. And once, when the Home Attendant lifted her to her side, with hands like grappling hooks, to remove her diapers, first thrusting with what seemed like unnecessary violence a towel inside her, ostensibly to clean her, I thought her beebee fish eyes were going to pop out of their sockets as her obese white belly huffed and puffed in complaint. At that juncture, Mr. Bohatir rushed to his wife's aid, shouting that the Home Attendant was manhandling her, and tried to help by imploring her to sit up. "Sophie, sit up. Sit up, Sophie." But that body had died long ago and little or nothing could be done for it, nor could it do anything for itself except fight back by its very death-like immanance against any living efforts to resurrect it.

But here's the interesting part: All the while this was going on Brodski didn't once close his eyes or blink them, or try to turn away or twist his dradle neck, if I would let him (which I wouldn't).

But when we were ready to leave, already in the door-way, and I was allowing, as I always do, Mr. Bohatir to recall the one and only image he has of his wife when he first met her in the "old country" wearing a sunflower-patterned golden dress and a wide-brimmed hat ("Oh, such a hat you never did see, Mr. Haberman") I could see Brodski craning that same neck when the Home Attendant got in his way to get a better view. Not having the heart to interrupt the old man's recount of his reverie, I continued to half listen to him and half observe Brodski. I tell you he wanted to stay. It was plain as day he wanted to stay. It was I who stood there refusing to see what my eyes took in. His dradle neck was so contorted as he made every effort to suck in one more last look that I even lost my place for a split second and slapped him across the face to get his attention. First time I ever did that. As you know,

107

that's not my way. But it just goes to show that even a man with as even a temper as mine can lose control of himself when sufficiently provoked.

Now what does all this mean?

I knew it! I knew it! You know what he did when we returned to the studio late this afternoon? He . . . *HE PAINTED!!!* That's right. The little ingrate sat there in his relaxation chair with a smirk on his face as wide as the counter girl's disgusting fat ass and he painted. And all I could do was stand there with both hands knotted behind my back and watch him. And, of course, it doesn't take much to guess what he painted this time. Any numbskull could figure that out—Mr. Bohatir's vegetable-wife; what else?! I tell you I never felt so humiliated and debased in all my life. Who's the idiot here? That's the question I keep asking myself. Here I expose him to . . . and he paints it!

Well, if it's a fight he wants, it's a fight he'll get. I said all along I prefer a strong opponent to a lackadaisacal foe. And I do. If he wants to put me to the test, so much the better. He'll find out fast how much of a warmonger I can really be.

Now let me see. I have someplace hidden away here in my notes something about this. Oh, yes, here it is:

HAVE YOU EVER SEEN ONE CHILD CHASING AN-OTHER? THE ONE IN THE LEAD, NO MATTER HOW AFRAID, IS ALSO GLEEFUL, MANIC. BUBBLING OVER WITH LAUGHTER AND GAIETY. HIS FEAR APPEARS MOCK. THE ONE BEHIND IS FEROCIOUS AND SE-RIOUS. THE HUNTER NEVER PLAYS AT HIS GAME. ONLY THE ONE HUNTED. IS THAT WHAT MAKES HIS PLIGHT BEARABLE? WE MUST DO SOMETHING, LIT-TLE ONE, MUSTN'T WE?

But I wrote that a long time ago, while we were still in phase one. Many things have happened since then. Changed significantly for both of us. I wonder if I can still count on it. I wonder? . . . No. I'd better not.

Here's what I have decided. Just as I once enlarged his universe, I now will shrink it to four-wall size. From now on he doesn't leave his room. He doesn't get to see one new thing, beautiful or ugly, outside. That's his punishment, let him paint from memory. From inside himself without inspiration. He stays locked inside himself from now on all the time. If I can't stay one step ahead of him in this tug-of-war of ours, then I'm not the man I claim to be.

Before I forget, let me make one thing clear. His painting of Mrs. Bohatir the other day did not miss a detail. Her stretch-marked rump; her obese white belly huffing and puffing in complaint; her frozen grimace of wonder. He even managed to capture those grappling hook hands of the Home Attendant and make you feel the ostensible violence they were perpetrating on his charge. But remember, I never once denied that he paints well. Even if I do project my own interpretations on his work, his craft and talent go without saying. Anyone can see that. That's not what I object to. If you think that about me, you don't understand me any better than Mrs. Knox does. I couldn't care less that he's an artist. Who cares about art anyway? It's his . . . it's his . . . *IT'S HIS UNBENDING BELIEF THAT HIS WORK IS AN ABSOLUTE END IN ITSELF THAT I FIND ABHORRENT!*

Since that day he was banished to his studio room, he has painted an entire collection of ugliness. At least that's the way these paintings appear to me. The bag lady with elephant legs; the epileptic slobbering at the mouth; the three-legged dog hopping, skipping and jumping along with it's one-legged master. I let him. That's my strategy

109

for the present. How much can he paint? How long can he go on? In his whole life he's only been exposed to so much ugliness. If my calculations prove correct, he'll run dry soon enough. A few more days, or at most a week, of this building up of his false confidence, letting him think he's got me where he wants me, and then, *boom*, his lights go out . . . forever. He's got nothing more to paint. There won't be anything to inspire him. Then we'll see who the artist is in this house.

And don't think he's done all this without malice aforethought. Even if he is an idiot and therefore deserves the benefit of the doubt, he's guilty. I should know. I tested him. The evidence in my favor is overwhelming. How else can you explain that only when I'm not there to observe him does he slip in a painting that isn't ugly? Like the Office Manager's Civil Service Lunch still life. It's true. The more tests I perform, the more I'm convinced he's only doing all this to spite me. When I left the room the other day, after placing a new canvas mat before him (actually he can replace canvases himself, but I did it just to hasten things up a bit because naturally, I can do it easier and quicker than he can and I was anxious to see the results of my test), that's when he painted the Lady With A Parasol. But get this: When I returned and took my customary place behind him to watch him paint, he gestured for a new canvas and immediately started out on something ugly: The Handsome Black Youth With the Intersection of Scars. And worse. A closeup still of his own feces. Now don't tell me that's inspiration. There's no doubt about it. Anyone who can paint that crap has got to be doing it to spite me. And he wouldn't do a stroke unless I watched him all the way. He made me witness every stroke until the blasted thing came to life before my very eyes. And when he finished, he smiled. Not a mere smile, but an artful smile, one graced with secret knowledge. It was not in pride at a job well done, his painting, but at the look he saw on my face. I did everything I could to suppress it, but how could I? I'm human. I've got to express my feelings even if he doesn't.

Well the time is fast approaching for his little artistic

flourish to peter out. And when it does, we'll see who has the last laugh in this house. He might have won a battle, as the saying goes, but I'm going to win the war!

I can't take any more of this. He goes on and on painting and all I've done for the past four weeks is sit here and watch. It's my world that shrunk, not his. At first I thought he'd fold up and quit when his ideas ran out, but I was wrong. He's long since stopped painting anything—beautiful or ugly—he might have seen in real life. Your guess is as good as mine where his inspiration comes from. It must have something to do with the way he's made. That's the only thing I can figure. Unless he gets his strength from his desire to beat me. Maybe that's what keeps him going. There's great strength in having a cause. I've always held that religious fanatics and artists have that much in common. They both have absolute faith. That's another reason why I detest artists so. One thing I do know. No normal person sees the world the way he does.

I've decided not to sit around any longer and wait. I'm going to take the initiative once again. It was a stupid tactical error to have given it up in the first place. Whatever advantage I had I lost. He's gotten stronger these last several weeks and I weaker. Every day he sits at his easel so contented and happy he reminds me of all I'm not. Right now he's in his most fertile period; four and five paintings a day. It's the ideal time to take myself off military pass and return to the war. As soon as I come home from the office today I'm going to institute a new series of punishments which should make up for the last four weeks and more. He's going to pay for what he's cost me a hundredfold.

Now: let me count the ways:

I take my adjustable shaving mirror from my medicine cabinet and place it before him so that he cannot paint a stroke without first seeing himself. The trick is to tilt the mirror to follow him regardless of the angle at which he twists his head. If he makes an effort to knock it away with his arms and hand prosthesis in a fit of frustration, I merely detach them. No explanations necessary, but let's see him paint without them. Like Narcissus gazing at himself in the pond, Brodski *must* look upon his own image. But he is not Narcissus. His squints, squeals, rocking motions to and fro in his seat, tell me that clearly. At one point he even tries to paint from memory. He shuts his eyes and makes every effort, but even though he can create in the dark, we both learn that he cannot do so effectually with his eyes closed. An interesting distinction here; perhaps, at a future date, I can do something with it. It takes him a full afternoon and much pain and effort to reach some sort of solution. Somehow, through what can only be described as a kind of self-hypnotizing technique, he learns to blank out his mirror reflection while continuing to look directly at it; in this way, by looking at himself as though he weren't there, the little bastard is able to paint. From his distant expression and the way he responded to my touch later that evening in the bath (he barely rose to halfmast), I doubt he was satisfied with the results. Didn't I once see a movie in which the concert artist knew before anyone in the audience when his music wasn't quite up to par? Even more interesting to me is the fact that he never thought of painting a self-portrait. If I were in his place, that would have been my way of adapting. Perhaps some things are too ugly to paint even to him. Or maybe, as I've suspected all along, he just lacks a Lautrecian sense of humor when it comes to his own appearance. That would really be a case of self-overcoming. In any event, tucking my darling into bed that night, I think I have made a good start in balancing the score for what he put me through and more.

Next:

Shine a weak-batteried flashlight in his face while he's painting. If he blinks, wiggles his head, gnashes his teeth in rage, aim it all the more closely between his eyes. Observe how his inner eye dominates. Like a Spartan, he stoically paints on. Affix a clamp light with a stronger illumination to his easel so the unyielding beam bores directly in on him without mercy. Watch him struggle this time even more assiduously than before. Pick up testimony attesting to this fact by the way he blinks unceasingly, even attempts to shield his eyes from the glaring light by making an effort to lift one arm prosthesis up to it while continuing to paint with the other. It must be the same as holding up a thousand pounds to him. He can only do so for a fraction before it comes tumbling down. In the end he surrenders. He closes his eyes. But ironically, just by giving in, he triumphs. His inner eye dominates. For when he opens his outer eyes he is able to paint on. Next take the theatrical spotlight off the wall. You know the one. The one heretofore reserved for his favorite painting, Munch's The Scream, when a reward was due him. Only now there's no reward. Not unless you consider his efforts to help himself—paint—under these circumstances a reward. But that's stretching it a bit, don't you think? No one takes the bible—"God helps those who help themselves"—seriously anymore. Fill the spot with the maximum wattage it will take till it's smoldering with heat. Hold it in his face for five, ten, fifteen minutes straight without letup. When I get bored or restless or am curious as to how he'll respond under different circumstances, I use my dimmer system and vary it a bit from low to medium to high. Take note: He is defeated. His inner eye can see no more. He can paint at no more than low to middling intensity. I am a trifle disappointed that he didn't reach high. The way he endured and struggled inspired me to root for him to do so. That doesn't make me inconsistent. I've always maintained I enjoy a good struggle more than an easy victory.

But even if he had done it, I wouldn't have given him a reward. No: We're not playing games anymore.

Buy some graph paper and three or four different-colored pencils. Tape-record a generous sampling of Brodski's classical musical collection; an even healthier portion of his neighbor's blaring disco sounds; and top it off with every metropolitan resident's midday buffet delight, the jamboree of N.Y.C. street sounds. Create a graph callibrated to measure artistic excellence (or its lack) in relation to the above-listed kinds of music and sound. Put earphones on Brodski's head and let him paint, making certain he understands that if he is to be allowed to do so, he must simultaneously listen to the music. Tunnel in the different sounds and groups of sounds to his retarded brain. First the classical music, then the disco, and last the honks, horns and screams of the city. Using a yellow-green colored pencil, collate to your graph as best you can his fine-drawn watercolor the classical music inspires him to create. Do the same on your graph for his sensuous oil color, which the disco sounds motivate, only now use a blood-red pencil, and note the San Francisco bend in your graph's curve indicating a distinct dropoff of artistic control and mastery. His jarring abstract painting prompted by the cacophony of city street sounds lends itself to like scientific measurement. You should hardly be surprised when this last work made up of punctuating slashes of line receives the lowest dip yet recorded on your graph, now signaled in by a three-pronged multicolored pencil.

Follow this by scrambling all three tapes together in a single-reel hodgepodge so that you have a cornucopia of whimsically discordant sounds; no sound, bar, note, belch or scream bears any relation to the others, or to any score that Brodski might previously have heard or even preconceived. After recording his response to this last reel on your graph in ivory black, look at it. Look at Brodski's paintings. A perfect correlation exists—from his first watercolor excelling in exquisite gradations of light and shadow and exhibiting meticulous draftsmanship, which received the highest ranking on your graph's scale, to the latest tossing sea of sounds causing a visual mishmash on his canvas, which was accorded the lowest rating possible. You can congratulate yourself, fellow scientist. You have captured in the most rigorous scientific manner the causal relationship between the ever-increasing breakdown of sound and the concomitant ever-increasing difficulties of the artist in overcoming it. Your graph's polyglot language of yellow-green, blood red, ivory black and three-pronged color has put to surgically precise number and scale all of Brodski's aborted starts, stops, jerks and slashes as well as any polygraph records the variations of its subject's body activities. Everything that is lacerating, contradictory, and unharmonious, either on tape or on canvas, is marked down and brought to chrystal-clear order on your graph for scientific posterity.

And I am the one solely responsible for it. My graph is even more telling than any of his paintings. Is this not incontrovertible proof that I am the greater artist/SCIEN-TIST than he? For I have orchestrated everything. He has merely reacted. My graph is a perfect poetico-scientific metaphor of the creative process in ruin. Of the artist's jumbled and jangled inner state when interfered with and blocked by alien and warring stimuli. I congratulate myself for this valuable scientific contribution. Next time, I pledge, I will do even better. There are many, many more independent variables to control, and I have only just begun to acquaint myself with my subject and his ego defenses.

How long will this go on? Until he gives up. Until his thirst is slaked. Until I break his will. That's what it's about, isn't it? His will. His need to create. He must stop painting. He must stop attempting to become more than he is. He must accept himself, as we all do, for the meat and potatoes and dead thing he really is. He must not aspire to anything. He must not want to do anything. Be anything. He must not remind me of what I'm not. What I forgot ages ago and never want to recall. He must reconcile himself to

115

live a life fixed, dead, ugly and inert. He must content himself with eating and sleeping and eating some more. He can't fuck. (Maybe he can. Maybe I should find him a partner, another limbless idiot like himself. It would be fun finding out if he can). Most important he must relinquish his need for beauty, which is what separates him from the rest of us and reminds us of our lack. Only when he learns all these things will I stop. And he will learn. As long as he's in my classroom and I am his teacher he will learn: I promise you that.

"He's not only an idiot," Caesar said when I returned home from the office today. He was responding to something I had said earlier that morning.

"Really," I said. "What else is he?"

"Well, for one thing he likes art, and for another, music. And I'll tell you something else. I don't like the way you're treating him lately."

I stood silent for several moments, rubbing the side of my face to collect myself. Then with as controlled a voice as I could manage under the circumstances, I asked, "What do you mean by that, Caesar?"

"I'm not Brodski. Don't play games with me," the Home Attendant answered. And then he gave a peremptory jerk of his head at the closet where I had locked away Brodski's prosthesis and special art equipment before he stalked out of the apartment.

Or was he peering at the Visual Mishmash, which hangs directly to the left of the closet door?

Caesar's response wasn't the only jolt I received today. At the office I learned that despite all the work I've put in getting my case records into shape, the real focus of the departmental investigation is field time coverage. Office tittle-tattle has it that the investigation is citywide and that it will be used as a basis to get rid of those employees not doing their jobs as an alternative to, or in addition to, proposed city layoffs. Special Investigations has put Rufus "Hatchet Man" Boines in charge and he's coming uptown next week to check out our field recording forms himself. If that's the case, I'm a goner. After thirty-four years I can kiss this job goodbye. There's no way I'll be able to make my W717's justify my field time after having spent all these weeks going over my case records thanks to Mrs. Knox. I wonder if she set me up. I wouldn't even put it past her to call my clients to see if I've been visiting them. Perhaps that explains her secret scribblings in her notebook every time she gets off the phone lately. And what about Rodent Face? When he told me the news this morning his little rat's face was exultant with triumph—you'd think Rufus Boines was coming to our office to escort him through the pearly gates personally. Come to think of it, Mrs. Knox wasn't so glum either. It definitely was a setup.

First thing tomorrow morning I'd better call the union delegate and ascertain whether I'm eligible for a pension if I'm fired.

And social security. Do I have to be sixty-five before I can start collecting?

Oh, well, I can always go on welfare.

It would serve them right.

Who? Who would it serve right?

When strapped in his relaxation chair in front of his easel ready to paint, it has become Brodski's habit of late not to utter a sound or otherwise exhibit any emotion. He knows full well what fate awaits him if he is to be allowed to paint, and he sets his mind stoically to the task. It is just a matter of what kind of punishment and how severe and how much time will pass before I initiate it. These moments prior to the punishment must be even more cruel for him than the actual punishment is. It is like having Damocles' sword handing over his head. He never knows when it will fall. On the other hand, I find these times of fear and trembling, specifically because they are unexpressed, delectable. So much so that I have gotten in the habit of stretching them from seconds to minutes to hours, according to my whim.

Still, just once, I wish I knew a way to break him of his stoical attitude.

When I aim my blow dryer at Brodski's backside when he's in his chair waiting to paint, the little fellow bumps and grinds in such a frenzy I could swear he was up on the latest dance craze. If I didn't have a dryer (actually I haven't styled my hair since beginning this final phase), I could just as well use an infrared lamp with a lever arm for this experiment, or even an electric heater placed under his chair. As it is, though, I am quite content with the hair dryer. In addition to watching him twist and turn his little ass to my heart's content when I turn the machine up full blast so the heat waves are concentrated on his tiny buttocks protected only by a flimsy integument of elastic diapers, I can also get a first-hand view of his face contorted into a thousand grimaces I'd never seen before. I note that the amorphous quality of his face permits him many more possiblities of expression than we normally made people have. But no matter how vigorously he thrashes about he never cries "uncle," or asks to be removed from his hot seat. Even though his chair's rubberized seat cover might be smoking, and I can nearly smell the burnt elastic of his diapers, the little bastard doesn't give the faintest indication of yielding to my will. He remains steadfast, gladly willing to withstand all the punishment I can mete out, just so he can paint, if I let him, later on. How do I know he's not just being stubborn? Something in the family of false pride. I don't. One can never be one hundred percent certain about these things. But I think I'm fairly safe in assuming that any special bravery on his part is due to love of his calling. After all, martyrs are not exactly unknown in the arts. There is an entire rogue's gallery of these foolish fellows, each literally killing himself for the sake of his art.

And finally, when I permit him to paint, it's as if he had never experienced the slightest discomfort. It's as if his brush were the one stepping on hot coals the way it flits back and forth on the canvas. With the frenzy of genius the little bastard makes one painting after another as if he were being paid by piece work. He has the appearance of one of those speeded-up cartoon characters, or Charlie Chaplin in his mad-dash walk. No Japanese assembly-line worker could do more. Perhaps I should contract additional Brodskis and go into competition with the art manufacturers of the world. Certainly in our age success in the arts is not so much a question of quality as of producing sufficient product and then mass-merchandising it. On second thought, one Brodski is enough. I am not greedy. I can accomplish all I need to with Brodski alone.

One thing more than any other annoys me about this experiment. Though the little bastard suffers before and after his painting, he never suffers during. When he is in the throes of creation, not as much as a single pained expression appears on his ugly face. It's as if his pain is suspended, in limbo; somehow he is able to block it out of his mind and save all his effort for painting. He never lets the pain interfere with or spoil the quality of his work. Only afterwards, when his painting bout is finished and I have taken him down from his throne, does he become human again and know what it is to hurt. I have to be careful here. The temptation is great and unwittingly I might cause him more harm than I mean to while conducting this experiment. In fact, the first time I executed it, Brodski couldn't sit on his rear for a week afterwards. Actually, he never really sits. Regardless of how I strap him to his chair, or which harness I use or safety bar, he just sort of lies there—no, *is* there—like a flower torn from its stem.

I absolutely love his helplessness.

Brodski's response to a block of ice planted under his rump produces pretty much the same histrionics as the hot seat does, except for one significant difference. The paintings produced because of the ice share one thing in common: A wintry look. I call it—his Cold Period. He paints what appears to me frostbitten landscapes: bag ladies, beggars and Bowery types warming themselves around a fire; children in the park sleighing. There's no such commonality of theme when he undergoes the hot-seat phase of this experiment. Not even a sunrise comes out of that punishment (although he's painted many of them before). Perhaps you can explain it; I can't. As for the rest of it, though, it's all the same. Even when it comes to the care I extend him. If it's not burnt flesh I have to guard against, it's his catching pneumonia.

I get some of my best ideas in the middle of the night. I force myself to rise and gather up my pen and notebook, which lie on the floor beside my bed, and jot them down. It takes considerable willpower to turn the lights on at this godforsaken hour; one truly has to be possessed. I hardly know what prompts such inspirations. But I know enough to follow them, nevertheless.

Poor Brodski. Somewhere between sleep and waking hours his fate is decided.

My brainstorm to strip Brodski of one of his paintings while he was still in the act of creating it serves as a sterling example of a punishment that came to me in the wee hours and pales by comparison all my other ideas that evolve out of slow and conscious deliberation. Thus when I attempted to punish Brodski by marking up Munch's print, or by using his own finished creations as old newspapers to cover the floors with, I hardly got a rise out of him. But when I yanked away from him his current work in progress and commenced to carve it up before his eyes, before the paint was even dry—nay, even before he had completed his last grandiose brushstroke—this proved more than he could bear. He sobbed inconsolably for hours afterwards. It was as if I had torn a baby away from its mother's arms.

And many other of my ideas conjured up in the nocturnal glitter have proved just as cruelly efficacious. Take my experiment dealing with his sense of smell. When I placed my large electric fan in such a position so as to let him get a whiff of his own stool, he hardly noticed. Regardless of whether he was constipated or suffered from diarrhea (and depending upon which punishment I mete out both conditions appear frequently now), or whether his bowel movement was regular (needless to add, very rare nowadays), the little bastard went on painting. But when I did the same with my own feces his fleshy nostrils quivered, and then clogged, and his breathing became so impeded I thought he was near gasping for his last breath. It was impossible for him to continue painting until I opened the windows and got the stench out of the room. But by then it was too late. His mood had already passed and it was time for his bath. The fact that I was equally revolted by his stink and not my own seems to me something for psychologists to speculate on. The "why" here doesn't really interest me. I think it's sufficient if I just describe my experiments as best I can and let others draw their own conclusions.

At least this time.

I've even found a way to break the little Spartan of his stoical attitude while awaiting punishment prior to being allowed to paint:

Place Brodski in his relaxation chair with no arm and hand prosthesis on, no easel and canvas before him, and let him be. He can go for hours without as much as twitching a muscle.

Next (moments after the first sequence), seat Brodski in the same chair with easel and canvas now before him, but still no arm and hand prosthesis attached. Watch the taut line on his cheek quiver, but still, no real sign of discomfort.

Finally (again, don't let a minute pass), seat him in his chair again with the easel and canvas before him and this time attach his arm and hand prosthesis as well as the pencil holder clasping a brush that is dripping with oil color. But don't let him paint. After five, ten, twenty minutes, observe his eyes, which are positively screaming with expression. His Stoical Response (S/R) is broken.

Don't repeat this experiment. It loses hold over its subject after the first time.

And finally, a stroke of genius: my electric shock experiment:

Wire an electric circuit through Brodski's universally adjustable hand-splint in such a way that his torso automatically receives a shock every time he touches the canvas with his brush. Sit him in his chair and, please, don't offer him any resistance. If anything, prod him on. The better he understands he's free to paint, the more joy this experiment will bring. The first shock he receives will be no greater than if he were walking on an electrically charged rug. He will jerk his brush back, stare bug-eyed at the canvas, as if contemplating an evil omen. Twenty to thirty seconds later he will try again. Same thing. Only who knows what he's contemplating this time? After half an hour, more or less, of numerous trial-and-error efforts, he will achieve a method remindful of a pointilist: dipping and dabbing the canvas with short, abrupt, pointed strokes, as if stepping between raindrops to avoid the storm. It is time to transmit a more telling message. Wire Brodski around the vulnerable parts of his body: his genitals, under his arm (arm?) pits, and place one live wire in the flabby folds of his neckless neck, just barely grazing his ears. One dab of his brush now and it's like all hell breaking loose. He is completely befuddled. Some evil force has taken over. How do I do what I do? It has something to do with these wires. He scrutinizes them but cannot fathom what. All he wants is to paint, and for once I'm not offering any overt resistance. If he can just figure out a way to overcome these wires, ropes, cords, these wriggling and writhing snakelike strands, he's free to paint. But how!? Should he give the canvas a soft caressing kiss of the brush? Nope! That's not it. The way his tiny torso was lifted from his seat, despite the straps, harness and safety bar he's in, tells him that. Then perhaps a jackhammer blow. Nope! Not that either. If anything his reaction was worse. He looked as if he was receiving a massive jolt of electric shock therapy. (He is). The little hair he has stood on porcupine's end. Good thing I put a bit in his mouth or else he might have swallowed his tongue.

At last, when he has nothing left, when he's drooping and sagging in his chair like a fish out of water, I disconnect the wires with an adroit, cleverly concealed flip of the wrist, and take his brush, which is still in the utensil holder, and guide it slowly to the canvas. Miraculously there is no jolt this time. No earthquake tremor. Just a streak of paint on his canvas, like it should have been all along. The way the little fellow gaped at me you would have thought I was God! The Devil! Or had the power to bring the two together. I couldn't stop laughing.

But don't get the idea that this experiment is flawless. Many independent variables, secondary motivations, and even a concept in experimental psychology known as generalization are not being given their just due. Despite its incompleteness, however, this experimenter is happy. I'm still laughing . . . even in my sleep.

Walking to the bus this morning I observed two young boys playing football. One boy darts out, feints to the left, then right, before continuing straight ahead for his TD pass. The other boy's arm is cocked but he never releases the ball.

"What happened?" asks the receiver, trotting in to meet his friend.

"That was fine," asnwers the quarterback. "I just can't throw that far."

What would happen if Brodski's brush couldn't reach the canvas? I decided to find out:

When I returned home that afternoon, after dismissing Caesar, I took out of the closet the deluxe exercise mat I had ordered months ago from the Abbey Rehabilitation catalog but until now had made no use of. Now I knew its purpose as if it had been preordained. I laid it before Brodski's relaxation chair. Then I walked over to Brodski's crib-bed where he was catnapping and lifted him from it. The little fellow sleeps all the time now. My experiments have taken their toll on him. While he was still fuzzy-eyed, I seated him in his chair but didn't bother to strap him into it or use his safety bar or body harness. I merely let him dangle precariously, following his natural body gravity. Then I placed the easel and canvas at a sufficient distance from him so that he couldn't reach them without having to lean so far forward that he would fall to the ground. The thought occurred to me that he might not brave this experiment. Well, there was no time like the present to find out. To my delight, Brodski persisted in trying to paint, but each time he did so, the damage was no more significant than if he had fallen on earth made soft by night rain or morning dew. The exercise mat so cushioned his landing that I couldn't in good conscience call it a punishment. It irritated me to think that he might enjoy free-falling through the air like that. The falls certainly didn't stop him from trying to paint. And that is the sole criterion.

I toyed with the idea of exchanging the deluxe exercise mat for the red-brick tiled floor on my patio. But that wouldn't serve my purpose either. For if Brodski went for it, he would break every bone in his body, if not kill himself. I racked my brains for a compromise. Finally I decided to try out my wooden floor indoors, but to buffer his crash by laying blankets and sundry bed materials on the floor. The image of a deserted building lot near the welfare center in Harlem strewn with jagged rock, half bricks, broken glass and tin cans kept floating through my mind. What I wouldn't have given to test Brodski there. But I knew the idea was out of the question. Suppose someone should see me. And how would I get his equipment there and back? No. My indoor punishment would have to do. It might not be as inspiring as the lot, but it would jar him plenty and let him know this was no holiday. To Brodski's credit, I must admit he tried. He even brought a smile to my face at one point when perilously leaning over but at the same time attempting to be cautious, he seemed suspended at a fixed angle like the Leaning Tower of Pisa. But finally he teetered and toppled to the floor. His thump was music to my ears. When I returned his painting equipment to the closet that evening Brodski heaved an audible sigh of relief. I don't recollect him ever doing that before. Progress!? Later on, in the bath, I examined his little body ravaged by welts, bruises, cuts and bloody wounds. And when I oozed ointment on his aching torn flesh to soothe the pain, the way he looked at me with the saddest eyes I have ever seen buoyed my spirits immensely.

Yes: Progress is being made.

I had no one to blame but myself for what transpired between Caesar and me the next day. In my haste to get to the office that morning after having slept late, I had completely forgotten about him. Of course this wouldn't have happened under normal circumstances. But nothing is normal in the Department these days. Department employees are being dropped from the payroll like flies swatted down. And I can ill afford another black mark on my record. Not with "Hatchet Man" Boines due to arrive any day now to start his investigation, and Mrs. Knox continuing to record my every move in her notebook.

"How do you explain this?" Caesar said the moment I walked through the door. And he pulled the blue-cotton hospital gown from Brodski's limbless torso, exposing his many sores, welts and wounds.

"I can't," I said, fumbling for words. "Other than the fact that I was trying to train him . . ."

"Train him!? You train animals," the Home Attendant said, hurling the words at me like stones.

"You *teach* human beings!"

The way he leaped to his feet, for a second I thought the Home Attendant was coming for me. I had already raised my hands to protect myself when at the last second he sidestepped me and headed for the door.

"You're worse than any idiot," he shouted.

"What could be worse than that?" I yelled back.

"A CRIPPLE!!!"

And he slammed the door behind him.

I turned now to face Brodski, who was still naked, his battered body shivering. As I bent down to pick up the hospital gown to cover him, a smile creased my lips. Poor thing, I thought to myself. I have to do everything for him.

Long before he set foot in our fifth-floor office it was known he had arrived. Someone said he had seen him getting out of a "spiffy" two-tone Eldorado with telephone, TV and bar. Another worker saw him waiting for the elevator on the ground floor. And Mother Earth confirmed all by pointing out that our Director had actually deserted his Botanical Garden habitat for the first time in years during office hours.

"But what does that prove?" queried Rodent Face.

"It proves he's here! The Special Investigator is here! That's what it proves!"

The murmers, whispers and stretched necks continued until A-37, who had been on the lookout in the elevator corridor, came rushing into the office shouting, "It's him! It's him!"

All quieted as our Director led the Special Investigator into the intake section at the front of the office. Every staff member sat with one eye glued to his desk and the other on him.

Rufus "Hatchet Man" Boines is a tall, erect black man with a perfectly rounded and shiny bald pate, a bushy mustache, and a somber no-nonsense air. He was wearing a white shirt, the collar stiffly starched, a paisley tie, a dark blue pinstripe suit, and his beige alligator shoes gleamed every time the light hit them at a certain angle, as did his manicured nails. The distinct fragrance of "a man's cologne," Brut or possibly Canoe, trailed after him wherever he went.

The Special Investigator strode through the center with the pomposity and disdain of a royal personage. Stopping

127

first at the intake section, he made comment to our Director about its workings. He mouthed a few platitudes to the intake supervisor as if he were a politician soliciting votes during a campaign. A client who had been burned out of her home with three children and was waiting for emergency placement caught his eye, and he walked over to her to inquire about something, but when she, in turn, was about to return the favor by asking him something, he waved her away as if he were a fine Southern gentleman and she white trash. He had little time to be bothered by clients. So what if some recipients suffered from a breakdown in the bureaucratic machinery? That was inevitable. It could not be helped. There was nothing he could do about it. As a whole, the system worked. It served multitudes. Besides, he was here on official business concerning a wholly different matter. No, he would not be diverted by secondary concerns. He knew his priorities well. Clasping the Director around the elbow as if to say "Let's get on with it," he drew him out of the intake section and through a door leading directly into my unit's floor area.

He was standing in clear sight of us all now, in the front of the office, with the Director, Tom Sanders, at his side, and though no one could hear what they were saying, we could see the Director smiling and pointing to our Office Liason's office, possibly offering it to the Special Investigator for his use. And when the Director gestured to a painting on the wall (probably referring to Becker's cancelled art show) and the Special Investigator launched into a smile of his own showing his pearly white capped teeth, I felt a peculiar kindred alliance with them.

It was not long before he accepted the Director's offer to commandeer Hans Becker's office, and while several workers (a maintenance aide and human resource specialist) busily set about carrying papers, folders, books, manuals and sundry supplies into it, the Special Investigator continued on his tour of Department units accompanied by the Director. After a perfunctory introduction he uttered a few words to each unit supervisor, perhaps mentioning what was expected of them, the

128

protocol he would follow (and tolerate), and every once in a while he deigned to glance at a caseworker. But he never said a word to us, never interrupted a caseworker from his work. It was evident he believed in the work ethic. For the most part his tour of duty flowed nicely, only now and then interrupted by an aide who would ask a question or relay a telephone message. Then the Special Investigator would stop him before the words were half out of his mouth and tell him what to do, order him one way or another to do this or that, without even seeming to listen to the lackey's words, as if his responses were ready made.

Three days later I was summoned to the Special Investigator's office. I was the first of the staff called. The Special Investigator had spent his previous two days at the center busily reading case records, going over field record forms, supervisors' performance reports, and had had at least one conference with each of the supervisors. Our Director, Tom Sanders, was also seen talking to him in private on occasion. Mrs. Knox was already seated when I arrived. She didn't bother to greet me when I entered. Our Director was conspicuous by his absence.

The Special Investigator inaugurated the proceedings by saying he gathered I knew why I was there. I had had the better part of two days to think about it and I was convinced of one thing: I would not give them the satisfaction of admitting to my own guilt. Looking him square in the face, I answered, "I do not." Out of the corner of my eye I could see Mrs. Knox seated in her chair, her fingers nervously drumming on her notebook. *I knew what was in that notebook!* The Special Investigator did not take his eyes from mine. There was an air of exaggerated solemnity about him. By feigning incredulity, he managed to keep me in the dark several seconds longer. He knew the power of that pose. The discomfort those few seconds caused me. At that moment I must admit I felt as much admiration as anger for him. Finally he said that he had selected me first since my record, from the appearance of my Supervisor's annual performance report, was the poorest in the center. And for a man who has worked for the Department for over thirty-four years, that really came as a surprise.

I answered that the key word here was "appearance." Other than the opinion of my Supervisor, who, as everyone knows, has always disliked me from the time I started in Harlem, what proof was there that I had either neglected my job or exhibited irresponsible behavior?

"For more than fifteen years to be disliked, Mr. Haberman? Why didn't you ask for a transfer? That would have been a simple enough solution." I shrugged my shoulders. There was no answer I could give him (or myself). The thought occurred to me more than once over the years but I had never acted upon it. Things weren't quite that bad, I kept telling myself. And what assurance had I that they would be any better in a new situation? With a different Supervisor?

"Still, we're not here to discuss personalities, Mr. Haberman, or to improve upon departmental relations. We're here to discuss your future with the Department. And based upon my findings and Mrs. Knox's *evidence*"—her hands were wrestling, tearing at the notebook now—"I'm going to have to ask for your dismissal."

I tried to respond to his words but I couldn't. I could barely digest them.

Quite the reverse, Mrs. Knox couldn't restrain herself any longer. "I'm not going to put my head on the chopping block for you or any other worker, Mr. Haberman. When I leave here I want it to be on my own. Not by dismissal."

By the way the Special Investigator ignored Mrs. Knox's acrimonious outburst it was evident he was not wont to give up the floor.

"At first, because you were only several months short of becoming eligible for your pension," he continued, nonplussed, "I had in mind only to ask for a voluntary leave of absence. In a year things will have blown over in the Department and you could have come back and started over again. Or perhaps we could have arranged for some special resignation status that would have left you eligible for benefits. But that was before consulting with your

130

Supervisor. All that's impossible now in the light of what she's brought forth. No, nothing short of termination will do now."

I was jarred. Stunned. Completely caught off guard. A decision to be made so quickly? So fast? My dismissal!? After so many years!? But even while in a state of shock more than a few arguments raced through my mind. One of which was my right to appeal. But at the very moment the ideas surfaced, I dismissed them. It was just what Mrs. Knox would want. She would give anything to see me squirm. To drag me through the mud. An appeal or its like would give her the supreme opportunity to testify against me in front of a board meeting. If it was the last thing I did, I would never allow her that. Indeed, that was just what she must have had in mind when she began compiling her evidence against me in the first place. A whiff of Tom Sander's jungle habitat scented my nostrils. As his office was adjacent to this one, I could smell the greenery. Where was he? All those years buttering him up with those infernal plants, and now when I needed him most, my trump. . . . Suddenly I realized how hopeless it was. How futile. There was nothing he or I or anyone else could do. My fate was lying on Mrs. Knox's lap. That was why my Director chose not to attend this meeting. It would have been as embarrassing for him as it was for me. Averting Mrs. Knox's eyes and with as controlled a demeanor as I could muster, I stood up to leave. But before I did, I made certain to take the Special Investigator's hand firmly in my own.

Mrs. Knox's notebook was still on her lap when the door closed behind me. She had not and never would get to read her "evidence" aloud. By all appearances she, if not the notebook or both, was bursting at the seams.

A half hour later I was sitting in a bar where I proceeded to drink myself into a stupor by late that night. One sentence kept repeating itself in my mind: *I've Still Got Brodski!* No matter how many feelings welled up inside me, no

131

matter how many thoughts too painful to accept swirled around in my head, I fended them off with: *I've Still Got Brodski!* The most terrifying thought that kept recurring over and over again in my mind and seemed to override all the others, the one that speared me on its killer lance and pierced my entrails was: If this job meant so little to me— or nothing at all, as I have told myself for so many years, as I have always believed—if I hated it so and placed no value on it, considered it demeaning, and worse, the ruination of my life—*Then why did it hurt so now? Why was there such overwhelming pain now when I had lost it? When at last I was free from it?* I didn't have an answer. Or if I did have an answer, I refused to face it. I fought it off. I've Still Got Brodski, I kept telling myself, *I'VE STILL GOT BRODSKI!*

I didn't want to know the answer. I didn't dare know the answer. I didn't dare equate the waste of my life, not with the job I had done for so many years, but with my reason for doing it. The real reason. My own cowardly, obsequious, fawning, impotent self. All those clients who meant nothing to me. All those 712's and case records and time cards and procedures and genuflecting to Knox every morning and cajoling the other workers every morning and burying true feelings every morning and getting up early every morning and not being late every morning and buying Knox newspapers every morning and filling out forms every morning and putting off my real life every morning and hating every hour, every second, every day of it . . . Why did I do it? What did I do it for? My life! The life I never lived! Could I make it up? How could it be made up? How could I have let it happen for thirty-four years?! . . . And now this. Nothing. No pension. No money. No way of getting my life back. Setting it right. Was I to blame. Was I respon . . . *I've still Got Brodski! I've Still Got Brodski! I'VE STILL GOT BRODSKI!*

On waking the next morning, in addition to a splitting migraine, I had a vague memory of collapsing on the street and being taken home by two policemen, one black, the other white. I recalled the black officer saying, "Sleep it off, brother. Anyway you look at it, a job's only a job. You're lucky. You still got your life!"

Even leaving the office yesterday for the last time proved unsatisfying. And I'm not referring to the "last supper" habitually given every worker who leaves the Department. That, for whatever reason, didn't come off. Not one of my co-workers took the initiative in passing around the brown inter-office envelope to collect contributions necessary to pay for the bacchanal. Of course, the only reason I wanted the party was to give me the opportunity not to attend. That would have been a fitting epitaph to my fifteen years at Harlem. More eloquent than any final words I might have uttered. But, as I said, even that satisfaction I was denied. The parting comments of my f-o-r-m-e-r colleagues rankled me almost as much. Not because of what they said but what they didn't . . . and the way they said it.

Richard Gould, for instance, his head down, his eyes averting mine, mumbled, "No more Knox." I could hardly hear him. It was his way of making light of a frightening situation. Of assuaging his own fear. I knew what he was thinking though: He'd be next.

Rodent Face: "Gee! It really happened. Gee!" Personal prayer answered. It was easy to figure where he'd be spending the night: at church.

Tom Sanders: Once again he was conspicuous by his absence. He did leave me a cactus plant and a brief note wishing me well, though. But where was he? He had seldom if ever taken off during office hours before. So why now? (Who could he trust to water his plants?) . . . Did he feel that guilty?

Mother Earth: She alone expressed something real. "You're the lucky one," she said. "Anyone who can get out of this crap, no matter how they do it, I'm happy for. More power to them." Seconds lapsed before she made her final comment: "They're all bastards!" And then she passed a stony glance in the direction of my supervisor's desk. She never mentioned a name.

My other colleagues and peers didn't say a word. Truth is they hardly noticed my leaving. On my way out of the building, while the elevator was descending, I broke out into a clammy sweat. For the first time in all my years in Harlem it dawned on me that of the thirty to forty co-workers who made up the fifth-floor office, I didn't know more than eight by name.

Oh, yes, Mrs. Knox. She never lifted her head from the new procedure she was reading.

When I returned home I was assailed by a new wave of apprehension. How was I to survive till I became eligible for social security? Seating myself at the kitchen table, I immediately set out to assess my situation. First I listed my expenses: rent, food, laundry, Con Ed, (there was no telephone; I had gotten rid of that cost as well as cable TV months earlier), entertainment, miscellaneous. Everything considered, my monthly total (including Brodski) came to $689.00. I needed twelve times that to make the year. A grand total of $8,268.00. Adding up my assets—bank accounts, checking account, contingency fund, cd's, money still owed me from the Department (back pay and money I had coming from my pension fund savings)—and figuring seven percent on my money, I was still short $111.00 each month. I cursed myself for not having readied myself for this dilemma. I certainly had had forewarning. Only a week ago or even less I could have applied for a loan at any bank or financial institution, the Municipal Credit Union included. But now it was too late. Still, there was no way I would ever return to work again. From here on I was determined to spend as much time as I could free from any constraints and entirely with Brodski. Nor would I reduce myself to applying for welfare. I wouldn't give "them" the satisfaction. Besides, I wasn't eligible anyway, not with the resources I still had.

In effect, there was only one course to follow: I would have to reduce my expenses to the bone. To begin with, Caesar would have to go. That would help considerably. As he hadn't shown his face since our last altercation, I only

134

prayed he had disappeared altogether; then I wouldn't have to pay him what I owed him. Knowing how peculiar he was in certain respects, it wasn't too much to expect. Mother also would be adversely affected. No longer would she receive gratuities for not making herself available. On the contrary, she could deem herself fortunate if she continued to collect her Home Attendant check. Hey! That was an idea. If it came down to it (and it did), I could divide the Home Attendant check with her. Why not? I was the one doing all the work. As for Brodski, he, too, would have to contribute. For one thing, there would be no more presents for him. No more excessive and irresponsible use of my contingency fund. And, too, I would immediately put him on a starvation diet (he ate little anyway) and restrict him to the clothes he already had. Perhaps on special occasions (if he did well on an experiment, for instance, or poorly) I would treat him to a new pair of diapers. To be sure, everyone would have to learn to deprive themselves if we were going to survive these hards times. If this was a test, I was resolved to pass it with flying colors. I would let no one and nothing stand in my way. I had waited too long. Now for the first time in my life I was free . . . free twenty-four hours a day to enjoy Brodski.

Here's an idea! I can always put Brodski on the street with a tin cup. Why not? He's got a visual advantage over the ordinary freaks.

Sell his paintings? NEVER!!!

. . . who would buy them?

"THE LORD GIVETH AND THE LORD TAKETH
AWAY!"

I removed the two pillows stored in my closet and placed them an arm's length apart on the deluxe exercise mat lying on the living room floor so that they paralleled each other exactly. I had purchased the pillows months ago from an elegant Madison Avenue art shop. It was my last extravagance and cost much more money than, even then, I had a right to spend. (Now, of course, for this final punishment, money is hardly an issue). The art dealer assured me at the time that the twin pillows were just what I was looking for. Handwoven and individually designed by a highly skilled Japanese artisan; maybe a hundred years old. "They don't do work like that anymore," he said smugly, his hands fondling the pillows. "They're as fine a pair as has ever passed through this shop. I really hate to part with them. But, well, business is business." I had told him I was looking for the kind of pillows a Samarai warrior might have used to lay his sword on, or, even better, to rest his knife on before plunging it into himself on that fateful day. Each pillow was intricately embroidered and had a beautiful picture on its face: one of a serene old man rowing a boat on a tranquil lake; the other of a woman, presumably the man's wife, strolling through her flower garden in front of their home. The pillows were made of the finest silk and each had golden tassels.

Next I awoke Brodski on the dot of seven—he was certain to hear the final chime from the clock I had put on the bureau next to his bed. Then, timing my strides to the rhythm of a Japanese song of sacrifice playing on a recently purchased pocket-sized tape recorder, I carried him from his crib-bed into the living room where the pillows were awaiting him. I had on a kimino and sandals (my version of ceremonial dress) and on my face I wore a more solemn and steadfast expression than usual. The previous night I had laid the deluxe exercise mat down and on it, now, in addition to the pillows, I placed the little fellow's body harness and chair so that he would be able to sit upright. All this was done prior to dispensing with any of his daily morning routine: before washing him, brushing his teeth, changing his diapers, feeding him, even before certain rituals he manages for himself (he does yawn regularly upon awakening and stretch himself; not his limbs, but still, he does stretch)—but even those I did not permit him this morning.

I daresay he knew by its very difference that this morning promised something special. That something was in store for him. But what? Then I let him sit in front of the pillows for precisely five minutes before placing a single object on each of them. One pillow held last night's leftovers from my supper; nothing he would normally eat: bits and pieces of hardboiled egg and scattered remains of shell. On the other lay yesterday's newspaper.

Neither object could possibly have held any special appeal for him. Neither had any intrinsic worth in and of itself. Past experience told me he would never notice either of them under normal circumstances. But nothing is normal about this final punishment . . . is it, little one? Brodski and I stayed there, in front of the pillows, for two and one half hours before he finally made his selection. Scantily clad, diapers soiled, shivering goosebumps (I had left the windows open), groggy with sleep, his eyes finally settled on the pillow containing the remains of my supper from the previous night. Hearing a thin plaintive sound emanate from him, I placed my ear to his mouth to assure myself that he actually was signifying some kind of choice. He was. I heard his stomach growl. I could not have asked for any better proof than that. I knew at once why he had selected the scraps of egg and shell instead of the paper. He was hungry. It was as simple as that. A reflex action. A physio-chemical response. I immediately removed the newspaper from its pillow and tossed it into the gleaming black garbage sack I had tacked to the wall directly to the left of the deluxe exercise mat, making absolutely certain

138

that Brodski's eyes followed my every move. Then I lifted him from his wheelchair, first unstrapping his body harness, and carried him to the breakfast table. After feeding him a hearty meal (the first good one he has had in days) I let him paint the rest of the day.

It is now two weeks since I inaugurated the final punishment. Every morning, at exactly the same time, in exactly the same way, like an ancient rite of passage that never deviates, I have repeated the ritual. On each pillow I place an object—each object holding precisely the same lack of interest, the same inconsequentiality, for Brodski. The objects might be as insignificant as a single match stick and a broken piece of lead from a pencil point, or an old sock with holes in it and a cantaloupe rind. Sometimes the objects are duplicates of each other: two bottle caps, for example, both Coke. The point is that Brodski has to choose one of the two. Why or which one he selects does not matter, so long as he selects one. As soon as he does, I pounce forth on all fours to remove the item, the one *not* favored by his smile, purr or quixotic gaze, and dump it in the garbage bag awaiting it like an all-consuming orifice. Once it disappears into the sack, the unfavored object is never seen again. Then, following my practice, I give him a hearty breakfast and for the remainder of the day let him paint to his heart's content. After two weeks I am certain he knows no more than this: Some kind of rigid malevolent pattern is unfolding. A pattern fixed and immutable, perpetrated by me, and as of yet not wholly decipherable. Except for the fact he must select one item over another as prerequisite to being allowed to paint, and the item *not* chosen disappears, he knows little else. For now, that is enough. My entire purpose these first several weeks has been to teach him no more than that. He can't possibly have any idea where all this is heading. He is much like a maiden being made ready for her virginal sacrifice. How pretty she looks. How nice the cleansing waters feel on her body. What an honor to have so much attention bestowed on her; the hair lotions, the body oils,

139

the slave girls. But even she suspects what's to follow after her fall.

Even if he does suspect . . . so what.?
All the better.

Thirty-five more items have disappeared from the household. The fact that not one of them has anything to do with art, is neither æsthetic nor necessary to Brodski's painting, does not lessen the impact on him. Brodski is beginning to understand that his world is shrinking—coming to an end! If only subliminally, he cannot help but realize this. Three days ago he stared—not really stared, but he did hold his gaze steady—at a gaping space in the corner of the room where a small bookcase used to be, and for a second at least, he winced in pain. Other signs, too, have recently appeared to hasten Brodski's developing understanding. This morning, for instance, when I went to wake him and carry him to the pillows, he was already up. Restless, with eyes swollen from lack of sleep. I derived a certain pleasure conjecturing what he might have been thinking during those early-morning hours. And then, at breakfast, he hardly ate with his usual zest; though he did eat. And finally, when I seated him in his chair to paint, what he painted also must be construed a victory for me, however small: a bare room with only a few sticks of furniture in it, the mood cold, barren, menacing. Of course the little bastard didn't compromise a stroke. Despite the fact that his subject matter was obviously influenced by his final punishment, he only seemed to try all the harder and in the end achieved what must be considered one of his finest efforts yet. Still, I am content: Regardless of how modestly shallow its depths might appear now, my foundation pit will assume infinite proportions later on.
Yes: This is only the foundation I am laying.

140

I have purposely not confined my selections for the pillows to objects from his room alone. Rather I have taken my choices equally, from the kitchen, the small alcove we call our dining room, and my own room as well. Because of this there is not a single place in all Brodski's world he can go where he does not perceive its emptying; where he cannot help but experience loss.

Lately I recognized a pattern unfolding whenever I placed a large and small object on the pillows in front of him. The little fellow invariably and without hesitation preferred the larger item. It doesn't take genius to figure out why. All things being equal (though many of the items were aesthetic, those were usually pitted against each other; if not, I certainly make every effort to give their rivals equal weight; and none had anything to do with his art), the larger the object, the more of an impression it makes when missing. A bureau, a record player, poster-size print, even an ash tray when taken from its accustomed space must leave what seems like a gaping hole to him. I no longer juxtapose large and small objects on the pillows. Instead, I pose large against large, small against small. My intention is not to make this final punishment easy on him. On the contrary, like a labratory specimen preserved in formaldehyde, I want to preserve him, draw it out, for as long as possible, enjoying each moment in leisurely draughts.

I am in no hurry now. We have plenty of time.

Sometimes I place two small objects to one large on the pillows. Sometimes three. I have on certain occasions gone as high as six to one. Never has Brodski selected more than three small items in place of one large. His maximum rate of exchange seems to be three.

The larger items I don't actually place on top of the pillows, but lay adjacent to the pillows' sides. Brodski makes his selections without difficulty. Whether the object is actually on the pillows or lying parallel to them makes little difference.

141

The cupboard is bare (literally). It is the first area in the household to have disappeared completely. Not that I had so many things in it to begin with, being a bachelor, but still, several of the items I did have Brodski placed great value on. His Matisse saucer and Picasso cup, for example. When he was forced to choose between these two, that was a sad day. Afterward he suffered a far greater indignity than merely having his appetite spoiled. Now, whenever he sits down to breakfast (he doesn't really sit any longer: the kitchen table has vanished, as have the chairs, and we both eat off the floor, me cradling him in my arms like a babe) the first thing I offer him is liquid refreshment. Not because he likes it so much but because it gives me an opportunity to use the one piece of kitchenware I did save from the garbage heap. An old rusted metallic army cup. Alas, Brodski hasn't taken a sip from it yet.

Since Brodski refuses to make use of his universally adjustable handsplint to aid him with his food these days, I have to mash it down his throat with my fingers. Otherwise he won't eat. I don't want him to starve to death . . . not yet, anyway. And since he no longer has an apron to cover himself with, most of what he eats, liquid and solid, seems to end up on his face or chest instead of where it belongs: inside him. When he finally is ready to paint he looks like a cross between an old army field cook who's just finished feeding an entire company of soldiers and the ster- eotypical artist indifferent to dirt. One interesting tidbit: You can hardly tell the difference between the grime, slop and grease stains left over from his food and the spots, blotches and oil color smears made by his everyday paint- ing.

And then always at the same time, in exactly the same place, I set the object before him on the pillows.

This afternoon after Brodski finished painting, he re-lapsed into silence. Your guess is as good as mine what he was brooding about. Unless, of course, it had something to do with what tomorrow would bring.

Now: Let's see. What should I select?

I know: The last of his art reproductions remaining: his favorite, Munch's The Scream. And as its companion piece: His Crib-Bed, an item, if not aesthetic, certainly large, functional and necessary to his bodily comfort for eight to twelve hours of his daily regimen (sometimes more). It is as integral to his "world-space" as any material item can be:
I'll give you one guess which item he selected to end up in the gleaming black garbage sack.

So now he lies on the floor amidst a spread of tattered blankets and stained sheets; without even the luxury of tossing and turning in his sleep. And when he awakes in the morning as one does from a dream that becomes too intolerable, he finds his nightmare not over, but con-tiguous with his waking hours. Everything he's dreaded and dreamt about becomes reality then.

This final punishment is proving well worth having waited for. There are so many things I can do with it. And of course I will do them all.

Then again, late in the afternoon after he's finished his morning's ritual and his painting for the day, and I'm standing on the far side of the room, my back to him, paying him no heed, completely absorbed by my own thoughts, thinking what's to go on the pillows tomorrow, or smiling over some earlier reaction of his, he sits in his relaxation chair glaring at the blank spaces before him,

143

angrily flapping his arm stumps against himself. And then, when I turn around unexpectedly to face him, the flagellation stops, but he continues to glare (now at me), arching his back stiffly against the chair, looking like anything but a defeated man.

It's taken weeks—months!—but every objet d'art, figurine, even his entire body of work is gone now. Only his painting utensils and equipment, relaxation chair, arm and hand prosthesis, and a canvas still in progress remain. He's been laboring over the canvas for a week, and even though his pace has slackened considerably, the quality of his work hasn't. The little bastard's as diligent and uncompromising as when he first began his final punishment. But this morning, little one . . . This Morning You Begin the Final Phase of Your Final Punishment. On the pillows before you you will find s-o-m-e-t-h-i-n-g n-e-c-c-e-s-s-a-r-y to your painting. And even if this "something" is only a start, a tease, a mere gesture, if my calculations are correct, it will launch the beginning of the end for you.

I can't wait to see your face this morning.
And how your painting is affected.

Now, let's see: What should I choose?

The item I selected was a tube of paint, half used, the oil oozing out. On the other pillow I put toothpaste, (Gleam), the container (sample size) as close to the shape and size of the tube of paint as I could find. The toothpaste, like the paint, was squirming out of its vessel. The oil color, Payne's gray, is one of Brodski's favorites. In the last month alone he's used it on almost every canvas he's worked on. But despite the fact that Brodski very quickly selected the oil color to stay over the toothpaste, his initial reaction was confusion. As if the little darling *never* reckoned on having to make such a choice . . . or did he, perhaps, reckon too much? Indeed, merely putting an object having to do with his art on one of the pillows seems to have triggered fears and trepidations in him. For certain, his entire day was ruined. Not only didn't he enjoy breakfast—he nibbled at bits and pieces now and then but he didn't swallow a single morsel, keeping the food lodged in the side pockets of his mouth—he didn't paint either. Or rather he did paint, but it was evident the effort couldn't measure up to his usual high standards.

What proved especially interesting to me, though, didn't take place until he was well into his painting. When, with his utensil holder, he reached for that same tube of oil color and began pressing it on the canvas, there was a look of innocent dismay on his face. No, more like appreciation. Gratitude. He was grateful. And all the time he was work- ing on his canvas, he refused to take his eyes off me, once even rotating that dradle neck of his the full 270 degrees when I moved out of his sightline. My guess is that the little darling was worried I'd take the pigment away from him. But I would never do that. It's not up to me to reduce his world. He will do that all by himself. I merely place heads under the quillotine. Brodski chops them off. Yes: Brodski is his own executioner.

This morning I offered Brodski what I considered an impossible choice, his utensil holder versus a favorite paintbrush. And it was. For the first time since his initial exposure to his final punishment he could barely make a decision. His eyes must have flitted from one object to another and then back again a thousand times over at least three hours, as if he were attending a tennis match, before he finally settled on the brush. Sidling up next to him on the parquet floor, I didn't utter a sound. Not a single word of encouragement. Despite his weeping, wailing, grinding

145

of teeth, and even an occasional glance of reproof at me, I feel it essential that he be left alone at this time with his thoughts. Even though I am only inches away from him in the midst of his ever-diminishing world, Brodski must come to grips with the fact that I will not resolve his dilemma for him. That regardless of which decision he makes, it is the wrong one; that there is no real solution.

He already understands that if his world is crumbling, it is by his own hands.

Of course, if he doesn't choose, he doesn't paint. There's no denying that. He must make a decision. No human being can untie the Gordian knot by shirking his responsibility.

And Brodski is human . . .

It never ceases to amaze me.

Brodski stopped eating a week ago; so did I. At first because I was toying with the idea of seeing how his hunger pangs felt. And then, simply becuase I lost my appetite. How could I eat anyway, buried in all this filth and shit? Puddles of urine around me and the most nauseating stench. And worse than that even . . . the way he endures. The way he drags it on. I would have thought his spirit would be crushed long ago. But it's not. He's still asserting himself. He's still painting! I tell you the wonder is I'm still alive after the frustrations I have had to suffer because of him. But I'll see it to the end. So help me. If it kills us both . . . I'll see it to the end.

He's suffering from vertigo. It began with debility followed by dizziness a couple of days ago; then a fainting spell in midafternoon yesterday, after he finished painting. And today he's lost his moorings altogether. It could be because he hasn't eaten anything for nine or ten days. He takes in only water, which I literally have to force down his gullet in the mornings, cupping it in my hands. but it may also be from lack of sleep. If he does sleep—and I doubt it—it's with his eyes open. During the day, except for when he's painting, they're closed. Of course, he always could paint in the dark. To an extent the same is true for his vertigo. When he's at his easel working on a new canvas, his dizziness hardly affects him. His head clears, he knows where he is. But the rest of the day he's useless. He lies there, limp in his relaxation chair, his head rocking to and fro, his tongue clicking, rattling his lower jaw, his torso slumping from one side to the other. It's a momentous struggle for him just to stay awake during those long afternoon hours.

But sometimes he's so weak, or his brain is reeling so, that when he reaches out to dab his canvas with his brush, he can't. His arm and hand prosthesis hang down like slabs of dead meat over the chair's sides.

The canvas must seem as elusive to him then as a small animal darting this way and that, to and fro, does to a child attempting to grasp it.

But after a short rest he gives it another try, mustering up even greater resolve and determination than before; invariably he's successful.

One thing's for certain: He won't give up. If I'm to triumph over him, I'll have to do it without his help.

Sometimes his vertiginous attacks are so acute he has no sense of time or where he is. Once while he was undergoing such an attack (even though it was late afternoon and he had completed his regular painting bout for the day) I rushed him in front of the easel and spun his relaxation chair around 180 degrees so that it was facing in the opposite direction of the canvas. He didn't even notice. When he made his effort to lift his prosthesis his brush was

147

stabbing at nothing but air. The next morning, though, his work reflected what he had gone through. The canvas contained a kind of whirling dervish effect. The more I think about it, the more certain I am that the little bastard put down his version of having lost all sense to time and place.

When evening comes and it's time for him to sleep, he doesn't have the faintest notion whether I'm waking him or putting him to bed. It's the same in the mornings. Only when he's painting is he alive. Like Lazarus he rises from the dead.

My job is to stop his resurrection!
And I will!
I must!

It can't be long now.

His utensil holder is gone
Work table (easel)
Table writer
Magnetic wrist hold-down
Plate positioner (palette)
Roto tray
Turn table

(He still has his arm and hand prostheses with their universally adjustable hand-splints and pencil holders attached to them, and two brushes, now screwed into the pencil holders like bulbs in their sockets. And, of course, his relaxation chair).

Body harness
Support vest
Oil cups and pans
Safety bar kit

And almost all of his canvases, varnishes, pigments, solvent thinners, canvas boards, stretchers, oil painting mediums have vanished also.

AND STILL HE PAINTS ON!!!

I know what I must do. I must take his relaxation chair away from him. It will be the same as divesting him of his skeletal structure. His supporting framework. With the safety bar kit and harness already gone, he'll be nothing but a mass of jelly without the chair. But what can I contest it with? It can't be his prosthesis. I'm saving that for last. If I need a "last." (If I'm correct about this, he'll quit before that). It's got to be something he prefers, needs even more than his relaxation chair. But what? I know; the seven canvases he has left. He'll never part with them. Not until he's used them to paint on (or tried). By selecting the canvases to stay, he'll reason he's insured himself another seven days of work . . . Of L-I-F-E!

Let's see him try and paint now:

After Brodski disposed of his relaxation chair this morning he forced me to splash water in his face because he refused to take a sip from the army cup I offered him. He knows I won't sully my hands any longer by touching his caked and sore-infected mouth. His intake consequently consisted of no more than the few drops he was able to lap up from his lips with his tongue. When I carried him from the breakfast area to the space where he paints, it came to me for the first time how weak I myself have become. Even though there's nothing left of him now but head (skull) and belly (swollen),—the rest of him, shoulders, chest, etc., has disappeared like everything else in the house—I had to exert all my strength to carry him. You can't imagine how relieved I was to finally have him seated in front of the spot where his easel used to be. He would have keeled over immediately had I not braced him by putting one of my hands on the small of his back. (Even that was difficult for me). With my other hand I held a canvas upright (almost too difficult), in that way affording him the opportunity to paint. But each time he made the effort to do so I would release the hand supporting him, and after wavering fractionally, he would inevitably tumble over and roll in his own filth. First in excrement, then in urine, later in both. He only made the effort once or twice, then he stopped. He seemed content to just lie there on his back peering up at me as If I were God. Looking down closely at him, I could swear he was praying. But more to the point, he didn't paint. At most, he made a few arbitrary strokes on the canvas; no more. And even more important, after a comparatively short while he gave up. He stropped trying. Even after I allowed a full hour's respite, he didn't try. Only then did I determine he had had enough. Being careful to avoid the urine and feces smudges he had on him, I picked him up (I definitely am weaker) and placed him in the corner of the room. And there he stays.

What is he thinking, I wonder.

Tomorrow morning, after the splotched canvas goes in the garbage heap and he's received his drenching, will come the real test. If he doesn't paint then: I win! Meanwhile he has all this afternoon and tonight to ponder.

All I can do now is sit and wait with him.

If you ask me, though, I'd say I've got him.

But still he might try. You can't be too sure. Not with him. I'd better study him closely this afternoon.

And when he opens his eyes tonight to sleep I'll see if defeat is in them.

Lips pursed slightly askew, he sits in the corner of the room, his back uncomfortably propped against two walls meeting each other at right angles, staring hollow eyed in front of him. He doesn't see me, he doesn't see anything. When I move my hands in front of him, left and right, up and down, his eyes stare unblinkingly ahead. And even when he perceives something, like a blank wall or a bare space, it is only an intrusion on him. A reminder of what once was and will never be again. He never whines. He

151

never purrs. Even his mewing sounds have ceased. He is so sad. Irretrievably sad. Every so often, at regular intervals, he bashes his conical head against the wall and his bulging belly quakes.

I wonder what he is thinking:

He didn't sleep tonight. Even though his eyes were open, I could tell. Silent sobs racked his body throughout the night, and then, when morning came, the weeping stopped. His body appears becalmed now, sedate. There is a serene look on his face.
Has he somehow prepared himself, I wonder.

(If he's prepared, I'm not. I need my sleep even if he doesn't).

I was wrong about him. He's not human. No one human could paint like this. On the floor without his relaxation chair and harness to support him, or even my own hand to brace him; falling over, toppling over, bouncing crazily like a balloon whose air is escaping; yet somehow managing, miraculously managing, to hold himself erect for the fraction of time necessary to dab the canvas before he collapses under his own weight again. And after using his last smidgen of oil color he paints with piss, shit, dust, dirt, pus, food remains, blood, biting his lip, anything to give him color; anything that allows him to paint; sometimes even mixing it all together in a compound on the floor to give his work an impasto effect. For four accursed hours I've watched beauty unfold before me as no man has ever seen it unfold before. As it never *HAS* unfolded before.

152

One stroke at a time. One momentous stroke. He sustains his ability to call forth all that is left in him, painting each stroke as his last, radiant, exultant with each stroke. His triumph is that of the man who knows the best in him is being expressed. Who knows what it is to be alive, really alive, in the present moment. What does it matter that he's going to die. He's lived as few others have. Oh, what I wouldn't have given to have lived like that. Even for a moment. Especially for a moment. Had I only known a moment like that, my whole life might have been different.

Brodski is eternal because he has lived . . . really lived in the moment.

Blank walls!
Bare rooms!
Wallowing in filth!
The foulest odor!
Starving to death!
Suffering from dizzy spells! Fainting spells! Vertigo!
Not a chair, bone, harness or hand to support him!
The knowledge he's going to die . . .

AND STILL HE PAINTS ON!!!

Four canvases left—

Three canvases left—

(I'm so tired I can hardly keep my eyes open)

Two canvases left—

His right arm and hand prosthesis, with universally adjustable hand-splint, pencil holder and brush attached to it, gone!

One canvas left—

(I have never been so tired)

Nothing! Zero! Nil! Blank! Void!

What's that? He's lifting his arm stumps? A smirk on his face? A beatific smile! He's . . . He's . . . in his own head HE'S PAINTING!!!

NOOOOOOOOOOooooooooo!!!